here

here

STORIES

HEIDI WICKS

BREAKWATER
P.O. Box 2188, St. John's, NL Canada A1C 6E6
WWW.BREAKWATERBOOKS.COM

ISBN 9781778530555
9781778530562 (ePUB)
A CIP catalogue record for this book is available from Library and Archives Canada.

COVER ARTWORK BY: Duncan Major
PAGE LAYOUT: Nadine Hodder
AUTHOR PHOTO: Nancy Beaton

We acknowledge the support of the Canada Council for the Arts. We acknowledge the financial support of the Government of Canada through the Department of Heritage and the Government of Newfoundland and Labrador through the Department of Tourism, Culture, Arts and Recreation for our publishing activities.

PRINTED AND BOUND IN CANADA.

Breakwater Books is committed to choosing papers and materials for our books that help to protect our environment. This book is printed on paper made of material from well-managed forest and other controlled sources that are certified by the Forest Stewardship Council®.

Canada Council for the Arts Conseil des arts du Canada Canada Newfoundland Labrador

SECOND PRINTING 2026

For my family, here and elsewhere.

CONTENTS

BUBBLES

Brenda is temporarily blinded as the spherical suds float through her open car window, moving at a snail's pace down the Trans-Canada Highway. Cat Power on the tape deck, traffic has been at a near standstill from the time she drove off the Argentia ferry. Hot drowsy day, air smelling of asphalt, the big bubbles seem surreal. Is she dreaming? Has she drifted off at the wheel? She floats her hand through the window, a bubble bursting onto her fingers. A boy, about ten years old, in the car next to hers, is in his own bubble, blowing bubbles. Hyperfocused on the bubble wand. Dipping it into the container, pulling it out, blowing softly, sometimes spitting in frustration—a baby dragon trying to learn how to blow fire.

She glances at the clock on the dashboard: 11:11.

That's an angel number, you know, Mom always said, growing up.

Brenda always thought angel numbers were bullshit.

Now Brenda, the next time you notice 11:11 on the clock, notice what it is that you're thinkin' about. It's the universe sending you insight about whatever's troublin' yer mind.

Brenda always makes a goddamn wish.

Bobby. Right now, she's thinking about Bobby. The crackly car phone rings. She's been given the company car to drive home with. Probably a "hush up now" gift from the boss.

Hello?

It's Bobby.

Well that was fucking weird.

Where ya to? Bobby barks from the other end of the line. Crunch crunch. It sounds like Doritos are falling out of the corners of his mouth.

I'm on the highway, Bobby.

Mom thinks you're gonna be here by noon. She got lunch on the go.

Well, I won't be there by noon. Traffic is at a deadlock. I'm barely through Placentia.

Crackle crackle, the phone reception in Newfoundland is not used to people with car phones.

Well, fuck, he says, don't leave me here alone for too long. Mom's cookin' cabbage and it reeks.

As a child, Bobby moved about the world with a curious nonchalance. Chubby cheeks, a dimple in the right one, a lid of golden curly cherub hair. Impish eyes that scrutinized. Gliding through the world, absorbing and devouring things that interested him, blocking out whatever didn't.

When he was five, a brand-new kindergartner, he refused to go into the classroom one day. The teacher had no idea why. Just flat-out refused to go in. Big Sis Brenda was called down from the grade six classroom.

Bobby, why don't you want to go in?

I don't feel like it, he said.

But Bobby. Brenda tried to be tender. Laid her hand on his arm. You gotta go to school.

Bobby didn't look at her the whole time. Stayed focused on packing his books in his bookbag. I know how to tie my shoes, what else do I gotta go to school for?

Brenda had suppressed a grin. She sighed. Look, Bobby, if you go in, I'll give you a loonie when we get home. Okay?

Okay, he slammed his locker shut and went directly inside.

Brenda! The two teachers who'd been puzzling over this situation beamed at each other, enchanted. Brenda's pride that day over their special connection implanted in her and it still grows. How did you do that? We've been here for thirty minutes with him!

I just told him I'd give him a loonie. She shrugged, shocked they hadn't thought of it themselves.

His hair is less curly now than it was in kindergarten. Cheeks less chubby. But Bobby's dry, humorous knack for shaking off shit is inborn. Sometimes his nonchalance rubs off on her and she likes it. It's a break from the angst she carries with her most of the time.

I'll get there as fast as I possibly can, Bobby. I can't drive through the cars in front of me.

He may have a one-up in insouciance, but she's still the older sibling and for that reason, still gets to play the parental card. She imagines him there on Circular Road now—sprawled out on the couch, feet planted on the ottoman, Mom calling out, What can I get you to eat there now, Bobby?

He's been living in one of the apartments attached to the house for years, but still spends much of his time in their parents' quarters. The only groceries he buys with his modest call-centre salary are Frosted Flakes and milk and hot dogs and ketchup. Carbs and dairy and protein and legumes. Wears shirts he's owned for twenty-five years.

The last time Brenda saw Bobby, six months ago at Christmas, he had on a grey ThunderCats T-shirt, with Lion-O standing broad-chested holding a sword, the other ThunderCats standing ready to battle, supporting his lead.

Oh my God, you've had that shirt since you were eleven.

Bobby just shrugged. So what?

It's literally falling apart, Bobby. It's a *rag*, Bobby.

It's a *shirt*, said Bobby. Who gives a flyin' fuck if it's got a few holes in it?

Maybe Bobby's the one who has it right. Maybe Brenda needs to get a Frankie Say Relax T-shirt. Worrying too much about work, up all night long, fretting about how people will criticize her, what she'll get wrong. Desperate for the acclaim she'd received the day she gave Bobby a loonie. She'd been feeling the buildup for several months before her boss advised her to take some time away from the office.

Levon, the colleague who'd recently transferred to Montreal, who she'd been having an affair with, left their Toronto office just after Christmas. The residue of guilt left a sticky layer over the sense of mediocrity she felt at work, about her life. She'd been eating too many Oreos on the couch in her mother's old Tina Turner tee.

Yet she judges her brother for giving less fucks?

The car phone rings again: Where are ya now?

Jesus, Bobby. You're dying to see me.

Shut up. Where are ya?

I'm just about at Whitbourne now.

The phone clicks. He's hung up, his attention likely back to a screen of some sort. Just like that. Moving on. Nothing to close the communication circle.

When she pulls into the rainbow-shaped driveway on Circular Road, Bobby is sitting on the front stoop, droopy eyes and a stoner grin glued on his face. The image will live eternally in her memory.

Nice shirt, says Brenda, throwing her bag over her shoulder and slamming the driver's door closed. She sizes him up, squinting her eyes. I don't see any holes or pit stains, wow. Looks like you bought it within the last five years, at least.

Bobby gives her the middle finger.

The second they walk through the front door her mother swoops to her side.

Brenda! She throws her arms around Brenda's neck. Plants a wet one on her cheek. Brenda smells some kind of sauce. We thought you'd never get here, girl.

Traffic congestion. Brenda returns the kiss. Pulls her in close and they are cheek to cheek for a few seconds. Her senses fill with kitchen smells. Bobby was right: the whiff of cabbage is undeniable. The scent penetrates into the fabric of her clothes and into her pores.

Dinner plates clink and clatter, four of them slapping piles of mashed potato and turnip and cabbage and pease pudding and salt beef onto them. Father dumps a full ladle of gravy all over everything.

Dad, honestly. That's gross.

Her mother pauses. Takes a moment to drink a glass of water. Exhales.

So, listen now. She passes the white wine around the table and Brenda sloshes her glass full and her mother shoots her the stink eye. The windows sweat with steam from the cooked dinner. We have something to tell you. We're selling the house.

Bobby drops his knife and fork and they clatter onto his plate.

Jesus Mary and Joseph, Bobby, watch it! That's your grandmother's china!

Whaddya mean, you're *sellin'* the house?

Listen here, says Fadder. I'm over eighty years old, I only half wanted to take on this house, I don't want to be at it no more.

Managing tenants, fixing up people's spills, tearin' up cat piss–covered carpets, paintin' walls covered in crayon marks and stickers. Every. Time. Someone. Moves. Out. Oh, he whines sarcastically, but it's a way to move into town, *Gerald*. Show the townies that us baymen aren't so useless as they thinks we are. Manage a little hotel, *Gerald*. We'll all help, sure! Come on now, *Gerl* b'y, they said.

In '65, after the politician moved out, Gerald's extended family put all of their savings together to buy the house. We'll share the responsibilities, they said. We'll slice the place into apartments, rent them to university students, they said. One main part of the house, and then stacked apartments on the west wing and in the attic. We can take turns living there if ya wants, Gerl. But you go first, you got the most skills. But you can *learn* us.

It never happened, of course. To make ends meet, at times they moved out of the main part of the house, scrunching Gerald and Judy and Brenda and Bobby, all four of them, into a smaller apartment, so they could increase their income by renting out a larger, more decadent part of the house.

The only time a family member stayed for any length of time was when Gerald's niece, Delia, moved into the main house with a bunch of her hippy friends. The four of them moved to the attic apartment and listened to the endless throbbing of music and smelled the eternal whiff of skunkweed that floated in the air.

Don't bodder sendin' me my portion of the profits while she lives there, b'y, long as you lets her live there for reduced rent, said Gerl's brother, Wayne. I wants to 'elp out. And keep an eye on 'er fer me, will ya?

Rarely was a thing changed inside the whole time they lived there. They weren't concerned with modernizing. But they kept it safe. Secure from the weather. The place had strong bones and thick skin.

It's a racket, said Fadder, dropping his forehead into the palm of his hand. Back-breakin' labour. Only thing I wants to dig a rake into now is these mashed potatoes.

We're movin' back home, says Judy. Back to the bay. This isn't a discussion. We're just letting you know out of courtesy, and she nods at Gerl, proud that she executed her lines just like they'd rehearsed. She turns her eyes towards her plate, eyebrows raised, blinking quickly, chewing quickly, sniffing and swallowing tears with her mushy peas.

Gerald shoots Bobby a hard stare. Now, we knows you're a smart fella, Bobby. I don't want to hear another word about it. Start thinkin' about your future. Now.

What follows is an eerie silence (outside of chewing and sloppy gulps of wine). Until Bobby slams his glass onto the table. Stands up and shoves his chair backwards and it falls over. Storms out of the room.

Brenda stands and takes Bobby's plate and her own.

I'll go talk to him, she says, and Mudder lets the tears flow more freely.

Brenda scrapes scraps into the garbage. Maybe she'll just offer him another loonie and be done with it.

He's already got his back leaned against the cellar door behind the stairs in the crawl space in the basement. He's got it done up with old lava lamps they found there when they moved in. A blue light bulb in the ceiling, a string of Christmas lights around the room. A Stephen Hawking poster. A Flaming Lips poster, a Pink Floyd poster. He has been sneaking down here away from his parents to smoke weed and think since he was a teenager. Brenda sits across from him and holds out her two fingers in a backwards V. Holding his breath, he lays the spliff in the cradle of her index and middle fingers.

Don't you care? he says.

About what? Inhale. Hold breath. The house? she croaks. Exhale. Cough, or ya don't get off.

'Course, b'y. The house.

Well, yeah. We've lived here since I was born. It'll be weird not coming anymore.

Brenda and Bobby had a magical childhood and adolescence in the house. Sure, they grumbled when they had to share a bedroom. But over the years, they'd gotten to know every nook and cranny of the place. Uncovered random artifacts in various rooms. An old crank radio that broadcast stations from who knows where or who knew when. A gavel. The lava lamps. When they moved in, a giant gilded mirror hung at the foot of the stairs, its gold emanating an aura of richness into the room. No one ever mentioned moving it, for it seemed as permanent a part of the house as its very foundation.

But you know . . . they *are* getting older, Brenda says. Dad's worked his ass off for years, Bobby.

S'pose. He has, indeed, worked his arse off. Bobby takes the joint. Inhales. Holds it. Exhales O-shaped rings. Does not cough.

And hey, maybe you'll like having your own place.

Bobby doesn't buy any food that astronauts can't consume, it is that processed. Most of his clothes are falling apart. But he does buy a four-thousand-dollar telescope that is perfectly positioned, peeking out the dormer window at the very top peaked gable of the mansion. Bobby covets the room. Dreams of moving his library up there. Decorating it the way he wants. Now it'll never happen. The books scattered in stacks on the cold floor around him range from a well-thumbed-through first edition copy of Hawking's *A Brief History of Time*—on top of his copy of Douglas Adams's *The Hitchhiker's Guide to the Galaxy* that Brenda gave him for his tenth birthday—to musician biographies and autobiographies to the Holy Bible. Bobby is a mystic in the guise of a skeet.

And how'm I gonna find a place like this place? How can you live anywhere once you've lived here?

The ghost stories Brenda used to tell him when they were little burst in her brain like fireplace crackles. That a woman lived in this cellar. She'd died here when she was pregnant, and now she just wanted a little boy of her own to love.

'Member when you told me, when I was a kid, a woman died here? Bobby says. You had me shitbaked for years over that. Arsehole.

I was actually *just* thinking about that when you said it. Brenda takes one last huff of the joint. She's well baked now. She hands it off to Bobby for him to suck and snuff. All sorts of people have lived here, for sure.

Died here, too. I have researched. During the Depression, this place was like a secret sanctuary for people who lived in the slums. And I know a lot of people—children and babies too—died during those years. Smallwood's offices were here for a good while. Like, almost twenty years. Rich families. The first person who brought cars to Newfoundland lived here. A Scottish asshole, from what I've read. And that's only the people who've lived here in our timeline.

Brenda wrinkles her brow at Bobby.

Oh? I know what you're thinkin' now, that I'm cracked, foolish, ol' out-to-lunch Bobby, smokin' too many draws. Just 'cause the multiverse hasn't been proven yet, doesn't mean it won't be. It's comin'.

Whatever.

You'll see. Sure, it's speculative now. It's only a matter of time though. Hawking theorized about it. Physicists generally just assume it's a multiverse we're in. It's a consequence of the current understanding of the fundamental laws of physics. It's not just some whimsical, romantic movie like *you* prob'ly thinks it is.

Oh, shut up, *Bobby*.

Shut up, *Brenda*. He gives her a playful shove.

Hey, maybe Mom and Dad will give us a big cut of the sale and you can buy a spot in Bay Roberts, or outside of town, or somewhere secluded. Think of the sights your telescope would see. You could really work on something. *You* could prove the multiverse.

Hmm. Bobby smiles. Maybe. He gazes off for a minute, looking serene, then snaps out of it. Listen, Brenda . . . I never told ya this because I figured you'd just make fun of me for it, or freak out or somethin', but . . . I've actually *seen* things in this house. Shadows. Felt breezes. Heard whispers.

The digital clock in the corner says 11:11. She's not really that surprised. More so satisfied. So . . . who or what have you seen?

Oh. Well . . . I've seen men wearing top hats and tails on their coats. Girls—housemaids or whatever, lookin' like they came from the 1800s, wearin' bonnets and aprons. Young men, in uniform, goin' off to war, their mudders' hearts broken, collapsing in sobs.

I wish you'd told me back then.

Oh, I told Shaun.

Bobby's best buddy growing up. Once again, his nonchalance relaxes her. I guess I get stuck in my own bubble sometimes, she says.

Well. He pushes himself up. Clear night. I'm goin' to the telescope room.

Can I come?

Nope. Not allowed.

Brief pause.

Yes, b'y, come on.

There is something ethereal about this room. Out of all the spaces in the house, Brenda is not surprised he chose the attic apartment to live in. The one closest to the stars. He has painted the inside of the window trim gold. On the floor is a Moroccan rug with an image of the three wise men riding through the desert on camels, another item left in the house when they moved in.

His face pressed into the telescope, Bobby murmurs, almost to himself, We're all in our own bubbles, Brenda.

Sitting on one of the wise men's faces, in her fuzzy state, she imagines Bobby floating through the window up into the stars.

But other people's bubbles are right next to us, he says, whether we're aware of it or not. And ya know, Brenda . . . in the bubble-verse, any one of our bubbles can pop at any time. Join with someone else's bubble. We could end up in a whole other existence.

THE ARISTOCRATS

Dawn whispers the day awake on December 24, 1925, Christmas Eve chimney smoke curling into the clouds.

From beneath the steep gabled rooftop with goldfish gills under the eaves, through the great dormer windows in the master suite of the Queen Anne Revival, Eddie and Marion Duncan blink their eyes awake. Marion wiggles out of the fine flannel on the flouncy, fluffy bed. Scuffs into her slippers and pulls on her dressing gown—red velvet garlanded with lace, ordered in from Paris last year. Marion cranks the radiator in the bedroom. Awake earlier than usual, she warms her hands. The help has not yet lit the fire that allows the Duncans to wake in warmth during the winter.

Why in't the fire lit? Eddie grumbles.

Hush now, dear, you just rest there, and I'll get the coffee going.

Why in't the girl doin' tha'? he barks. Where is the girl?

Ellen starts at six, dear. It's only five yet. Why don't you go back to sleep?

A sturdy, reliable work ethic is a trait of Eddie Duncan's lineage. His clan, after centuries of churning rocky soil and stealing and selling sheep in the Scottish Highlands, eventually moved to the Australian gold fields and then to a small port town on the St. Lawrence River called Montreal, where Eddie was born. Many Scots immigrated to this part of Canada, seeing opportunity in the vast, forested land. His father became a co-founder of the Canadian Pacific Railway. Eddie was lucky to even get eye contact with him. Never a ruffle on the head, or a "good job, boy."

They moved to Newfoundland in 1890 to develop the Newfoundland Railway. He was fifteen. Boy, his father said, yer old enough now ta earn yer keep. It was the first time he remembers his father looking at him. He began to get attention for the first time in his life. His father brought him along to meetings. Don't mind tha' boy, he'd say to his colleagues. He's here ta listen and learn. He won't make a sound. Eddie would stare at the floor. Well? Boy, don't be rude, say hello. His father would smack him in the back of the head in front of the other men, and he'd look up, turn beet red, wave. His father let him balance the books, whipping or hitting him if he got something wrong. The sting of it on his knuckles, the zing of betrayal each time he was stricken . . . he still feels it, any time anything goes wrong. Success is money, money is success. Everything outside of that is failure. Poverty. Filth.

Marion's family immigrated from Lebanon in 1880, when she was five years old. Her father operated a photography studio in St. John's, where she would assist when she wasn't at school. It was here that she met Eddie for the first time, when he and his brothers came in with their father to have their portraits done. The doom Marion felt when coming face to face with Eddie's father that day implanted deeply. As she led him towards the portrait studio, he glared at her, *through* her, with an intense sternness that made her feel like there was an evil spirit in the room. From that day forward, any time she was in his presence, she felt the same paranormal shiver.

Eddie and Marion's courtship didn't begin until years later, in Bannerman Park, on a lazy Sunday afternoon. Marion rested against a tree, her well-loved copy of *Little Women* cracked open before her.

Eddie approached, shyly. Wha're yew doin' here? He wasn't as gruff back then as he is now. She wasn't quite sure what to make of him. She'd seen him around school, roughhousing with his friends. There was a solemnness about him. He rarely smiled, and yet, she sensed in him a yearning for connection. Sometimes they'd catch eyes passing each other in the hallway, and his frown would soften. He'd almost smile, but would then catch himself and look quickly at the ground.

Oh, just . . . getting lost, I suppose. Marion glanced from the pages up towards his face, playing coy.

Whas yer book abou' there?

Oh, this—this is my favourite. It's about the lives of four sisters who look out for each other and cheer each other on.

Ah. He kicked the dirt with his boot. Sounds nice.

Here, she held up her hand, why don't you help me up? We can go for a little walk.

He took her hand and it felt softer than she expected it to.

Yer hands, he said, they feel tough! He jabbed her gently.

Well, I don't just sit around reading books all the time, you know! I help in the kitchen, washing and cutting and cooking, I clean the floors, I bring in wood . . .

Well . . . He took her rough hand in his smooth hand. If ya don't mind me sayin' it, a girl so lovely as you deserves all the privilege in the world. He kissed her hand. I don't care how calloused yer hands are.

She warmed inside at these words and that gesture. She snuggled in and they strolled, arm in arm, through the park and around St. Thomas's church, down King's Bridge Road, back towards

Bannerman Park. They talked about their families, their upbringing, their aspirations.

We're eating our food tonight, if you'd like to come over? She laid her hand on his arm and held her breath while he answered.

What's *your* food?

Traditional. Lebanese—shawarma, hummus, pita bread, baba ghanouj, manakish with minced lamb . . . You've never had anything like it, I promise.

Eddie liked spending time away from his own family. The Gosines always welcomed him with open arms and plenty of food. He fell in love with Marion from across the dinner table.

They married in 1900, Eddie's mother supressing sniffles, his father standing with the same callous expression he wore like a uniform.

In 1904, Eddie and Marion obtained the first ever car imported to Newfoundland. Eddie had endeavoured to establish the automobile industry as a branch of the railway. The ridiculously massive vehicle clanked and clattered around town, an object of gargantuan curiosity to the many onlookers, agog at the wealth that sputtered down Waterford Bridge Road—barely a road at all. Twigs scraped the sides of the car, getting caught in the wheels. Chugging along at a peak speed of twelve miles per hour, the Locomobile was seen as intrusive to many locals, spoiling crops with its obnoxious exhaust fumes.

Over the years, farmers complained about the noise, which tended to make their horses skittish. In 1918, a local paper, *The Workman*, declared,

The life of the average pedestrian in the City (St. John's) *these days is one of perpetual peril. Let him attempt to cross a street, in broad daylight, and he is lucky if some auto doesn't come around the corner, at a rate of 15 miles an hour, and just miss him by a scant foot, while the chauffeur glowers at him as much to say, "Get off the earth you lobster! What right have you to be on the street?"*

Ach! Eddie's father snapped, Let 'em complain. Peasants. They dunno a thing about economic development.

Seventy-four Circular Road was a majestic nine-thousand-square-foot Queen Anne Revival with gabled roofs, an asymmetrical floor plan, twelve-foot ceilings, gilded mirrors imported from Paris and a sweeping staircase showered in a crystal chandelier from Beverly Hills. Eddie and Marion moved in, not quite believing the gifts life had afforded them. Marion made toast and coffee and eggs for her husband each morning. Waved from the door as he drove off to work.

His father had been seized with pneumonia on his way back from Europe, and his health had been deteriorating since. Eddie sat next to his bed as he took his very last breath, clutching his heart, his eyes wide, terrified, his mouth agape, looking as if he was sliding straight into hell. Despite his riches, he was a man at war with himself.

For years, Marion and Eddie tried to conceive. At first, Eddie was sensitive.

S'okay, my love, let's be patient, he would whisper in her ear and rub her shoulders each month when her period came.

But when a calendar year had passed, Eddie began to feel a low broil in his guts. His father's voice, bouncing around his brain, condemning him for failing to produce an heir. He noticed his fists clenching. His jaw tightening. It became a constant state for him.

Marion noticed when the words of comfort, the soft gestures, faded into nothing.

It came, she said.

Ah, he said.

His brow turned *V*-shaped. Intercourse became infused with frustration.

When two calendar years had passed, Marion suggested, Maybe it's just not meant to be. Eddie's guts, by now, were at a rolling boil. Bubbles popping and splattering on his insides. He punched the wall and stormed upstairs and sat on the bed and pulled his hair out and hit himself in the face. Trapped in a maelstrom of self-hatred, he only spoke to Marion when necessary after that. He channelled all of his energies into his work.

Imagining that he would be having more dinners at the house, with plans to branch out into the electrical industry, he deciphered that Marion would not be able do all of the traditional cooking *and* keep the house in proper order all on her own.

Don't forget to write "must understand plain cooking" in the advertisement, Marion, Eddie said, slurping his coffee, the morning he delivered the news that they'd be hiring help. Make sure that's in the advertisement, now. He crunched his toast, reading the paper, avoiding eye contact. I want her to be able to help you as much as possible. Toast crumbs stuck in his moustache. Some fell onto the newspaper. Somewhere in his mind, getting a housemaid was a gift to Marion. An apology for not delivering.

Marion's insides glowed, more than they had when they'd first started trying for a child. The sensation shocked her. She sensed an opportunity. Marion did not include the requested add-on for the ad. Truthfully, it did not matter if the girl had plain cooking experience. She could teach her that. The girl needed only a fresh attitude and a friendly soul, accepting of education. Marion wanted someone to clean, but also to provide companionship, someone to whom she could provide protection and guidance. She wanted to guide young women, braid them into the community, thread them into the businesses she was helping to establish. Dry grocery stores, restaurants, confectioneries, a theatre, hotels. The work her family was doing with the Duncans' developing electrical company. That she did not and would not have her own children brought her infinite melancholy. She vowed to herself to work with the young women to lay the groundwork of tomorrow.

WANTED—*Immediately, a Girl for housework, good wages offered; apply between 6 and 7 p.m. to* MRS. E. DUNCAN, *74 Circular Road.*

Ellen was the thirteenth candidate. Yanking the giant front door open, Marion saw a young woman of small but striking stature standing before her. Ellen's large brown eyes glistened with hopeful desperation. Her hands clasped in front of her, shoulders slightly slumped, she carried an endearing nervousness and wore a Mona Lisa smile.

Marion laid a hand on the girl's shoulder, accompanying her into the sitting room. Where are you from, dear?

Mudder 'n Fadder shipped me out from Placentia, Ellen said. Fadder don't make enough money to feed us all, so they needs me to work to send money home.

Marion made a mental note to arrange for dialect and grammar lessons.

Well, dear, if you work for us, you'll meet that goal. Now. She motioned towards the chesterfield. Please have a seat. Would you like a glass of milk? Or tea?

Oh, no t'anks, missus. I'm fine. She folded her hands on her lap.

What's your name?

Ellen, miss. Ellen Murphy.

Oh, that's a lovely, classic Irish name. You can call me Mrs. *Duncan*, please, dear.

Oh, yis, Missus Duncan.

Now, Ellen, do you have any experience cleaning?

Well, I sweeps and picks up after the youngsters all the time. I got four younger sisters 'n brudders. I cleans dur diapers, washes dur clothes . . . das just a few things.

We have a Chinese laundry service here, so you wouldn't need to worry about doing laundry.

You got any youngsters, missus? Ellen squinted, curiously. Missus *Duncan*, I means. Sorry. She looked at her hands on her lap and wrung her fingers together.

Marion looked down at her own hands. No, Ellen. We don't have children of our own.

Oh. Well . . . I can chop and cook potatoes, bake bread, mix up cereal, if das any help.

Yes, certainly it is, Ellen. Marion breathed a silent sigh of relief inside, anticipating Eddie's question: Can she understand plain cooking, Marion?

Ellen, what do you see yourself doing when you're older?

Well, missus, if I were to get this job, I'd be happy to just do this for as long as I can. Take care of me family, but also gets away from 'em too, know what I mean?

Marion laughed. Yes, I grew up with a big family myself, she said. And even though it's just Mr. Duncan and I now—she looked around, making sure he wasn't near, and then leaned close to Ellen, as if telling her a secret—I could use a break from him sometimes too. She winked at Ellen, and the girl covered her mouth with her hand to stifle her giggles.

But Ellen, Marion continued, can you imagine if you could do something besides this? What would you do?

This question truly flummoxed the girl. I haven't thought about that, missus. Her big brown eyes smiled, and Marion saw the glimmer of possibility, the sparkle of imagination, and that was all she needed.

How long have you lived, Ellen?

The girl looked confused. You mean how old am I?

Yes.

I'm fourteen, Missus. *Duncan.* She put her forehead in her palm.

It's all right, Ellen, you'll get used to it. Ellen, would you like to be our girl?

Yis, Missus Duncan. I'd like that very much.

Standing at the stove, the hot pot boiling rapidly, Marion pours the water over the ground coffee in the jug. There is immense pressure on this afternoon's business lunch. Eddie has been working on this deal for a year and is trying to secure the signing. He's getting up there in years, and things haven't been going well. He needs this.

Marion is coordinating a traditional Lebanese lunchtime feast for twelve hungry men. In the fifteen years since Ellen joined the household, the staff has grown to include three others—Mabel, Shirley and Sarah. Together, the team of women has executed countless business lunches. This one has to be more perfect than the rest of them.

The years have not been kind to Eddie.

When Marion tries to pinpoint a particular moment in time when he became completely sour, she can't. Not really. It happened in increments, over the years. The frustration and devastation of not conceiving a child was the first chop at the tree. There would be times when he would still kiss her, but to her it felt steely. Vacant. She believed that the ridicule he still endured from his father manifested into resentment towards her. She worried that it was her fault. What could she have done better? For years, Marion overcompensated. She felt her husband's pain. The failure he felt with each scold from his father. Each time she had to tell him she had gotten her period. She reminded him of all he did have. The home they lived in. The respect they got from the community. Several successful businesses.

But Eddie only became increasingly isolated over the years. Stewing in his office on the third floor, grumbling any time Marion spoke to him. Secretly, she wept, feeling herself a failure.

On more than one occasion, she walked into the room to see Eddie standing too close to Ellen. Watching her clean the floors. Standing behind her, whispering in her ear as she polished the banister.

I felt 'im breathin' behind me even before he was close. The first time it happened, I'd been workin' there about a year, I dare say. Most of the time he was cold. Standoffish like . . . barely even looked at me, like I wasn't even there. Even that, truth be told, made me feel . . . wort'less. But this one day, I was polishin' that big ol' creepy mirror at the foot of the stairs, and I caught him in the reflection. Standin' there, in the doorway, holdin' the folded-over newspaper in one hand and his coffee in the other. He was leaned against the door frame, and I saw him just starin' at me. Eyes all squinty. A hungry kind of look in 'em. And when he saw me notice him, he just kept starin' for a second or two. Like he wanted me to know he was noticin' me. Then he just looked back at the paper and strolled away. The shivers down me spine that day, oh my. I was 'fraid to even say anything. 'Fraid he'd hear me. I never knew he was takin' any notice before.

Second time it happened, he came even closer. I was doin' the floors that time. Down on me hands 'n knees. You missed that section over there, Girl, he said. Pointed to the corner of the porch. I scrambled me way over there, but he didn't leave when I did, just watched. Make sure you get all the dirt, Girl. He was so gruff 'n grumble all the time.

Third time it happened, that was the first time I felt his awful breath on my skin. Polishing the banister, I was. He was walkin' down the hallway towards the stairs, and he brushed right up against me. He paused for a second and I felt his hotness, comin' from his mouth and also his groin. I froze in place. Waited for him to leave.

I shuddered any time Missus Duncan left the house.

It was after the fourth time it happened that I told the other girls. He'd grabbed my hair that time. Pulled my head back and kissed me hard on the neck. Whispered in my ear, I don't want ye here, but if ye must be here, Girl, you'll earn yer keep. I felt his hardness against my back. I couldn't hold back me tears.

He ever do anything like that to you? I asked Mabel, her arm around me, wipin' tears away. She was older than me. I was fifteen then, she was twenty.

No maid, never. Would ya tell missus?

I . . . I don't know. She's so good to me, I don't want to upset her.

My Jesus, maid, sure ya knows she'd look out fer ya. Sure, she treats us like daughters. You especially, you were the first.

Yes but . . . she wants to protect the peace, too. What could she do?

She could make sure yer never alone with him . . . not leave the house while he's home . . . she'd do something, I just knows it.

There were versions of Mr. Duncan all over town. Men, walkin' around in their top hats and their suits with tails, their shiny shoes, their moustaches, combed just so . . . takin' whatever they wanted. How could us women compete with those men? They held all the power. Makin' us feel like trash. Subhuman. Men out home weren't like the men in St. John's.

Fifth time it happened was in the porch again. I was bent over and he'd come over and was hoverin' behind me, about to do somethin' awful, and thank merciful Jesus, the front door open and in comes Missus Duncan like a guardian angel. Mister leapt back at the sound of the handle. I was 'fraid to even look up.

Eddie? she says.

He only walked away.

Dear? she says, at me. Are you all right?

I nodded, trying some hard not to cry. Later that night she came to me. I was finishin' the kitchen, about to go to me quarters.

Ellen, I want you to know I'll never leave you alone with him again.

Guardian Angel.

For several months after Marion witnessed the moment with Eddie, poor Ellen's nerves were wobbly. She quivered whenever she entered the main house from the servants' quarters, which exited into the main upstairs foyer at the top of the great, grand, winding staircase. Fearing what was on the other side.

Witnessing it broke Marion's heart in a whole new way. Shocked by what she saw and felt in that moment, she felt she was looking at a stranger, and an immediate resentment towards her husband grew within her right then and there. Even when he wasn't in the room, she felt his energy, floating, threatening, inches away from her pores, just waiting to seep into her sense of peace. Always on guard as to where abouts he was. She locked the servants' quarters at bedtime and hid the key so he wouldn't creep through the walls in the middle of the night. She began sleeping in the room next to the master bedroom.

Marion felt so free when he was out of the house. When Eddie was at the office on Water Street, she would practice dinner service with the girls. Placing the soup dishes, twisting them thirty degrees for presentation. Remove the bowls, place them on the correct side of the sink in the kitchen. Deliver the entrees within five minutes of the appetizer dishes. Wash the bowls while the men eat. Desserts garnished and delivered. And always make sure the men's glasses are never empty. The girls had the routine to a precision. Countless dinners over the years, mastered to perfection. Their dinner parties became known.

Inwardly she was repulsed and terrified of him. But she never let on to the public. She kept up appearances. The order of things inside 74 Circular Road was tense, smooth, and ready to burst.

While Eddie was at work, Marion attended suffragette meetings and instructed Ellen to go do errands in town, in case Eddie made a surprise visit home during the day. She took on a leadership role in the chapter, and when she returned home at the agreed-upon time, she spoke to the girls about what they were advocating for. The right to vote. Protection against domestic violence. Maternal health. Marion gave speeches in government offices that she practiced on the girls at home, in front of the gilded mirror, the girls cheering her on from behind.

Eddie gritted his teeth when his business associates made mention of Marion's public speaking. Somewhere inside, he wanted to support her, but he could not access that internal thread for long enough to grasp a hold of it. Anger shrouded his insides, coated him in a thick, black tar that turned him into an ash-covered volcano, smothered by constant feelings of inadequacy and bubbling rage.

Above it all, hovering around him, a veil of loneliness. Desperate to feel . . . something.

The maids are up at 7 a.m. on Christmas Eve. Marion has already lit the fire and made the coffee.

You had the wood piled nicely, Ellen. Wonderful work, dear. Made it a cinch to get the fire going.

They work together in peaceful silence through the morning. Peeling potatoes. Chopping carrots.

Noting that it's nearly 10 a.m., Marion asks if the other maids are up. Time to start setting the table and cooking the lamb.

I'll go tell 'em to start at the linens. Ellen brushes her hands on her apron and rushes off.

Marion has noticed Ellen's nerves relax significantly in recent years, since Eddie has given up on her. Her skittish ways have softened. She observes, though, how the air stiffens whenever Eddie is present.

At precisely 11:35 a.m., the maids are lined up perfectly, their uniforms pressed to perfection.

BOOM BOOM BOOM! The heavy knocks come to the door, and Marion and Eddie rush to greet the guests. The men bobble in, removing their coats and dropping them on Ellen's outstretched arms. She teeters under their weight and carries them to the cloak room off the porch.

No rest for the weary, hey, my man? Henry Waterhouse, a prominent colonialist, slaps Eddie on the shoulder. Doing business on Christmas Eve, ay old boy?

Gentlemen, Marion says, arms open. Welcome to our home. She takes her seat next to Eddie. The only woman at the table.

Money. It's the only word she hears from them. The same one word, over and over and over again. Money. Money money. Money money money money money. Twelve bobbing heads, twelve mouths flapping, a cacophony of sounds popping and barking in the air, each trying to speak above the next, burping and quibbling, none of them listening to another, only listening to themselves, the goal quite simply to look impressive and to acquire things. They slurp their brandy, devour their lamb. Slop labneh onto pita bread. Gobble the meat, gulp it down, drink some more.

Everything is going smoothly.

A loud clatter from the kitchen.

Eddie tenses, frowns towards the kitchen door. Marion lays a hand on his knee underneath the table, hoping the bitterness she feels towards her husband doesn't pulse through her fingers and give her away. But he is unaware. She feels him relax. For him it's the first time she has touched him in years. Service continues without a hitch.

Slurps.

Pour me another!

Cigars in the parlour.

Slaps on the back. Shakes of the hands.

Bless yew and yer famileh! Eddie is as jolly as Ellen has ever seen him as he closes the front door behind his last guest, swaying out onto Circular Road into the Dickensian falling snowflakes. A merry Christmas to all!

Eddie stumbles from the door into the parlour. Come 'ere, yew. He wraps his arm around Marion's waist and plants a wet, sloppy kiss on her cheek and pulls her along with him. It takes everything in her not to yank herself away from him, but she fears his reaction.

Girl! he yells. Fire! Light tha' fire!

Ellen freezes, thrown back in time to when Eddie was more vocal. Years ago, around the time when he . . . She prays that another one of the girls will come out of the dining room.

Girl! Eddie bellows.

The others are cleaning the dishes. It has to be done immediately to have space to begin preparing the turkey for the next day. Another twelve hours of work ahead of them. Eddie's and Marion's entire families are coming for Christmas Day dinner.

Ellen scurries into the parlour and lights a match.

Good job tonight, Girl, Eddie grumbles, plunking himself onto the parlour sofa and dragging Marion down with him.

Thanks, sir, she mumbles. She senses his dark energy behind her, standing, stumbling towards her, his scrawny hand reaching out.

Marion leaps to her feet. Eddie! Don't you dare lay one hand on her. Her name is Ellen and you will respect her. Stop calling her "Girl."

Eddie's skull feels heavy with the devil's drink. He looks blurry eyed at Marion, past her, into the gilded mirror from Paris. He blinks at the reflection—his long-dead father staring back at him, his eyes black. He pushes Ellen to the side, and she topples dangerously close to the fire. Eddie lurches towards the mirror.

Marion rushes to Ellen and takes her by the arm and they watch Eddie carefully. He inches his face closer to the mirror until his nose touches it. He mushes his face into the glass, raises a hand to it. He sobs, wet tears and mucus streaking and steaming the mirror. Marion can't remember the last time he was anything but sullen. She and Ellen grasp each other, unsure of what to do. Slowly, Marion releases her grip.

Eddie? Dear?

He continues to sob. His head hangs low. He clutches the mirror.

Are you all right? She takes a step in his direction. Another step. Another, her tea gown floating behind her. It's unnerving, seeing him cry.

Suddenly he stands straight. Remembers where he is. Wipes his face with his sleeve. Whirls around to face her, and she gasps at the look on his face. The Eddie she fell in love with is gone. A ghost. Stop! He holds his arm up. Don't come a step closer.

Eddie, it's all right. Marion's heart aches for her long-lost husband. Decades of pain, broiled up inside him, thorns and brambles infiltrating his very being, every moment of every day, imprisoned by expectations and the need to provide. He heaves his body towards her, his jaw clenches, his brow crumbles into rage. He extends his arms and encircles his hands around Marion's neck and squeezes. All he sees in her existence is failure. Failure to become a father. Failure to achieve the same level of success as his father. Failure to make her happy.

Ellen's pulse races. She is an ensnared rabbit. Her eyes flit around the room until they land on the fire poke. Marion grasps her husband's hands and looks deeply into his eyes, praying for recognition, a connection to the past, to the days they went on walks, hand in hand, through the park. But any remnants of the Eddie who sobbed into the mirror have vanished. His eyes are black. Vacant. Possessed by ghosts.

Marion lets her hands slip off his hands and down to her side. Her breath is short and quick, inhale, exhale.

From behind him, Ellen raises her arm in the air and brings the pointed end of the poke down hard, sinking it into the top of his skull.

The earth halts on its axis. Blood trickles down his forehead and cheeks and he collapses, first to his knees, and then into a heap on the hardwood.

Marion herself falls to the floor, coughing, gasping, crying. Ellen rushes to her side, her arms around her.

Missus Duncan, Missus Duncan, oh my God, Missus Duncan.

The two women stay there, in a lump on the floor, Eddie right next to them. Mabel, Shirley, Sarah have scurried into the parlour at the sound of the thud, and they shriek at the scene in front of them.

Marion pushes herself to sit.

Ladies, quickly. Help us here, please. Let's just . . . roll him this way. The women look each other in the eyes, and just the one glance confirms what they knew was happening but have never spoken aloud. They've each had their moments with Eddie, when they've been made to feel threatened, unsafe, worthless.

The women work together, wordlessly, just as they've done dozens of times over the years, for dozens of dinner parties, silently, knowing just exactly what to do.

That evening, the smoke billows from the chimney and curls into the clouds as the women share a fine bottle of port.

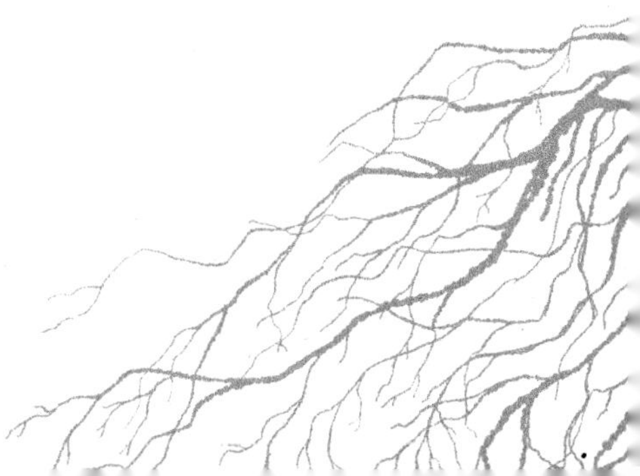

SIX CENTS A DAY

Their shoulder bones, brittle from malnourishment, crack on contact as they slam themselves, over and over again, into the English oak doors of the Colonial Building. Finally, they burst inside—hundreds of them, thousands more outside—ripping portraits of the men in power off the walls and snapping them over their knees, pounding their fists on tables and flipping them over. Every window in the building, shattered.

They seize an upright piano from the dining room, pitching the ornate candelabra on top into the corner. Haul the piano outside and shove it down over the front steps, keys clanging, hammers inside bouncing on the strings. Drag it into the park. Torch it. Flames lick the wood, spitting wild, angry orange strokes into the black sky on April 5, 1932.

Inside that building is where Squires and his government planned the food rations made necessary by the Depression. Rations that provide half the nutrition a human being needs. Half of what they themselves are eating, no doubt.

The *Evening Telegram* declared that government would provide for each family of four:

25 pounds of flour,
1 quart of molasses,
3¼ pounds of fatback pork,
2 pounds of beans,
1 pound of split peas,
2 pounds of corn meal and
¾ of a pound of cocoa.

Six cents a day they were surviving on. Barely. Life on the dole.

There! Ellen screams. Around the side! Get him! She shrieks it into the crowd until her throat is raw. The protestors dash, ferocious, clawing to get to the prime minister of the Dominion and rip him to shreds.

It was Black Tuesday, October 29, 1929, when Marion's illness took a turn for the worse. Ellen sat next to her four-poster bed. She ached to embrace the woman who'd become her mother and mentor, cruel contagion a deathly blockade. For the mites of disease to be floating in the air around them to invade this woman's kind, generous, change-making body was an injustice. Surrounded by blood-spattered handkerchiefs on the night table and bedspread, Marion's influenza had become pneumonia, turning to sepsis. Her body, desperately trying to heal itself, killed itself instead.

The stock market crashed, and Marion lost consciousness and left this life, taking a piece of Ellen's soul along with her.

During their years together, Ellen had worked her way up to manage the housekeepers, accompanied Marion to suffragette meetings, and eventually taken on a significant role as an administrator and researcher, an active participant in the Ladies' Reading Room—a space where women poured over the best newspapers around the globe and discussed society's issues.

The settlement from Eddie's death had paid off the house, free and clear. Marion had signed it over to Ellen early in her illness.

I want you to protect this house, Ellen, Marion had said, squeez-ing the girl's hand. Ownership is freedom. It's very novel for a woman to own a house. Protect it fiercely.

Ellen vowed that she would.

Most of the housekeeping staff returned to their rural communities after the market crash took their jobs. Rural families received even less than the St. John's dole because they had more space to grow their own vegetables.

Ellen, Mabel, Shirley, and Sarah, the original four housekeepers, were the only ones who remained in the house. They'd become a family, having learned to work together over the years with a rhythmic, cajoling efficiency, ending each day with tea by the fire. They helped one another through life, just like the March sisters, each on their own path but supporting the same cause.

In the years following Marion's death, their cause shifted from women's rights to human rights. To demand more government support for unemployed families, they gathered signatures, wrote and distributed newsletters, armed themselves with hard knowledge and spoke with passion at meetings in the House of Assembly, continuing the advocacy work that Marion had instilled.

The March sisters have had to be creative about justifying their existence, which they do by renting the apartment around the side to visiting British Members of Parliament who need a place to rest in between visits and negotiations with the local government, which regularly visits homes, to police food consumption. Since they're employed, the women are not eligible to receive the dole.

Now, isn't this house owned by the Duncans? they were asked repeatedly.

No, sir, Ellen would respond. As I keeps tellin' you every time you comes to call, I've had the deed signed to *me*. It's right here. She jabs her finger at the papers. The house is paid for, and it's owned by *me*. So. Leave us alone now, please, sir.

Fierce.

The March sisters discuss the state of things every evening around the fire, usually continuing the discussions had at the Ladies' Reading Room.

You know . . . thinkin' back . . . when that devil Squires was driven out of office for bribery, it was like God was lookin' out for us, Ellen says one evening when her tea is a hot toddy.

Many world newspapers supported suffrage, but Squires had always resisted. Three women ran for office in the 1925 election, Marion and Ellen key to the campaigns. But none were elected. They spent the next years gathering twenty thousand signatures for the next election. Squires was found guilty of redirecting funds to pay himself and was asked to leave office.

Then Eddie Duncan died that same year, Sarah says.

Yes, girl. Ellen hiccups, whisky-giddy. The twenties were wonderful.

The tightening of her chest that grasps her whenever Eddie's name is mentioned is softened with booze. Since that fateful night in the fireplace, his white face, stern and pointy and gaunt, has surprised her in the mirror at the foot of the stairs. There, a spectre floating in the shadows, then gone again.

You ever . . . *see* him? she'd asked the other maids.

Shirley nodded. I do. Least . . . I thinks I sees 'im from time to time. Or . . . I *feels* 'im, lurkin' around, in the dark, watchin' but pretendin' he's not, like he did when he was alive.

He was always more focused on you than anyone else though, Ellen, Mabel says.

You know . . . Sarah stares into the fire, tossing back tea. Him and Squires, two o' them got the same cold look in their eyes. Like death. Ever notice that?

Yes, maid, indeed I do, says Mabel. Like they got no emotion. No empathy.

They just feels so . . . entitled. Takes whatever they pleases. The only one who matters is themselves when it comes down to it, says Shirley.

Women certainly don't matter, not really, Sarah adds.

The poor don't matter, Ellen says. She has learned how to snap herself out of the freeze state whenever Eddie haunts her. Her thoughts control her now, not her fears. Something happens inside, when those old feelings come. She conjures the many talks she had with Marion, empowering her to use her mind to outsmart the men. To master the art of control from a higher plane than their brains are able to function from. Let them think they're still the ones in command.

And Squires now, back in again, Shirley adds. A proven felon. How's it even allowed? A politician to run, after he's been proven a fraud?

Like we didn't already know he was corrupt, even before he was removed from office for bribery, Mabel says.

Yet here he is, the sleeveen in power again. And as if the dole is all the government can afford to give, Ellen huffs. *Yes*, now. Not for one *second* do I believe that.

The women have walked through the central slums of St. John's. West of Circular Road, weaving through Georgestown, Hayward Avenue and Barnes Road, across Merrymeeting Road, towards Central Street. New Gower Street. Carter's Hill, an area that began to sprout after many lost their homes in the Great Fire of 1846. Decrepit, insanitary conditions. Children, made of skin and bones and sunken eyes. Malnourished. Surviving on fire-hydrant water. Night-soil men using rudimentary dippers to remove human waste into barrels, the dwellers of the homes never escaping the smell of desolation. Some homes had no floors. Holes in the roofs. Most were not weatherproof. The city's plans to demolish the area and build affordable housing were sidelined by the market crash. Boards falling off the sides, dropping onto the ground, rotting into nothing until they rejoined the earth along with all of the other death that had preceded them.

Take them, please, for the love of God, begged some mothers, holding their crying babies up in the air.

None of these people have work, said Shirley, that night around the fire. They've all been laid off, they aren't given enough food to survive.

Yet government has managed to double the police force, Mabel snorted.

Yes. Amazing, isn't it? Sarah stared into the fire, hoping some new insight would reach out to her from the crackling sparks.

Their rations run out a week before renewal time, said Ellen. How's that supposed to work?

I mean . . . Shirley wrapped her hands around her cup. This'll sound insane, but . . . how many do you figure we could keep here?

Well . . . Ellen looked up at the extravagant ceiling as if the thought hadn't occurred to her before, relieved one of the other women had vocalized it . . . From my rackets with city council,

I knows the slums got two point five people per bedroom. London County Council recommends a maximum density of one point two five people per bedroom. Our house got ten bedrooms plus four other apartments, and we stretch it by a bit because so many of the humans are youngsters, and babies, and our bedrooms are big . . . I figures we could probably keep . . . thirty people livin' in the house?

It'd be crowded, said Sarah, more to herself than anyone else.

There's got to be five thousand people in the slums, Ellen said. City says seven hundred and fifty houses needs to be demolished. So yeah. *That's* crowded.

If we can help any, well then that's something. Mabel watched Ellen's face lift. Ellen didn't know that Mabel secretly stayed awake at night until she knew Ellen was sleeping. Ellen didn't know that Mabel felt so very fiercely protective during the times Eddie preyed on her. Moreso than the other women. In a sharper way than Marion even. Ellen didn't realize how strongly Mabel felt about her.

Maybe we could rotate who stays here, said Sarah. Clean them, feed them, let them sleep, then have another crowd come in. You know? One crowd at a time.

There'd have to be rules, certainly. Things can easily get out of hand, agreed Shirley.

No one can come in if they're drunk. Or are particularly disease ridden.

Yes, we can't cause more damage than there already is. We have to stay healthy.

And we have to make sure the Brit don't hear anyone come in. God knows now what he'll do.

We'll sneak them in during the night, when the Brit is asleep.

Through the back door, on the opposite side of the house that he's on.

And that was that. The beginning of the covert operation.

On their next walk through the slums, Ellen crouched down next to a mother with an infant and two other children under the age of five.

Listen, she whispered, passing a loaf of bread and bag of potatoes. You needs a wash and a good sleep and a good feed for you and your youngsters. We can help you out if you keeps it quiet. We don't want any trouble. We just wants to help people where we can.

The woman's eyes widened like saucers. The first ounce of hope she'd had in years.

Yes? Ellen held on to her shoulder.

Yes. Please, missus, the mother said.

Someone'll be back for ya after dark, Ellen said.

The March sisters grew rhubarb and Chinese bean sprouts in the basement by digging them up just before the first frost and simulating springtime with candlelight and heat. This trickery allowed the remaining preserves from last summer to line the walls of the cellar—blueberries, pickled beets, bakeapple, potatoes. Lentils, from the connection they've maintained with Marion's Lebanese community.

Ida Marie and her children three became new people during their time at the house. With each mouthful, their eyes became a little less sunken, their cheeks a little more rounded. The look of desperation on their faces losing some of its edge with each meal, sleepful night and proper wash.

Ellen taught the oldest child, Teddy, how to play "Hot Cross Buns" and "Mary Had a Little Lamb" on the piano. Marion had taught her those simple melodies that provided such instant gratification and safety. Mabel told them stories, acting them out, dancing around, sometimes pulling Ellen in for a do-si-do, and they laughed just as children should laugh. Shirley taught them simple arithmetic. Sarah performed healing rituals on them, as her father had back home when she scraped her knee or had a cough.

Miss, said Ida one day, as Ellen carried sacks of flour up over the stairs, I wonder if . . . She wrung her hands as she gathered the courage to ask.

What is it, maid? G'wan, tell me what's on yer mind, Ellen said.

Well, my cousin . . . her husband, he just passed away, see. She got four youngsters. Older'n mine. They're smart as anything, they could help . . .

Yes, my dear. We've got space. Just be sure to keep it quiet, all right? We don't want to cause any trouble here.

Ida's eyes brimmed with tears. Thank you, miss. You don't know what this means.

Now, now. Whatever we got, we shares. We'll get through this. Don't you worry.

The next night, Ida's cousin Carrie creeped in the back door with her youngsters, two boys and two girls, aged fourteen, twelve, nine and eight. The older ones ate more than the little ones already there. Shirley's arithmetic classes became more complicated.

Now, we're gonna need help with baking bread and preparing meals, Mabel said.

Not a problem, ma'am, Ida and Carrie both said. Anything we can do to help. Anything at all.

I, uh . . . Carrie said. I don't suppose you'd consider . . . my husband's sister, Erin. She's got her own five youngsters. Two of 'em are young, like Ida's baby and her youngest. Older three are eight, ten and twelve. They can help.

Soon the house was full. The servant's quarters, all the bedrooms, the living room, the dining room. Inside the house, people became happier. More relaxed. Fed. Cleaned. Rested.

The March sisters' secret operative functioned largely out the cellar, weekly, after everyone in the house was sound asleep. Creeping downstairs to the secret garden in the darkness, they crawled through the door and weaved through the underground tunnels, holding their breath when they reached their destination, waiting a few minutes, every time.

Sounds clear, one of them whisper-hissed to the rest. When they felt sure, whoever was leading hoisted her shoulder against the door in the floor of the Colonial Building, popping it open into a sprawling pantry packed with food. The women loaded ingredients into bags: extra flour, potatoes, cornstarch, fatback pork, cocoa. As much as they could fit, from the back of the pantry where it was less likely to be noticed as missing. They always made their journey the day before they knew the import ships would be docking at the harbour. Mounting the sacks of food on their backs, crawling back towards their own house, they'd stack it into their own cellar, bringing enough upstairs to bake bread, peel potatoes, chop rhubarb, boil lentils.

In one room, the women sewed dresses and shirts out of flour sacks. To battle the Depression blues, the companies had begun to sell flour in bags with pretty patterns.

In the kitchen, the women pounded bread dough each morning.

I hates this brown flour, Ida said, on more than one day.

Tastes like poverty, don't it? Carrie replied.

At first, overhearing a comment like this would prompt Ellen to surprise the house with a jar of blueberry preserves. Until they started to run out.

At first, the women and children who came to the house were bursting with gratitude and joy. They would bring loaves and other supplies to their neighbours in the slums, taking a roundabout route through the woods so that they wouldn't be discovered by the police.

Each time they returned to the house, a new name whose family needed refuge was mentioned. They started to run out of space.

Ellen called a house meeting one afternoon. We've been running out of room, as you all must notice, she said. I propose that we start alternating spaces. If some of you would return to your homes to open up for spaces that others might need, it would be appreciated. The other women and I have spoken about possible solutions within our control.

Well, are the four of ye gonna take turns?

Well, said Mabel, this is *our* home.

Well, said Carrie, the most outspoken of all the mothers, we feels like it's our home now too. If we're sharin' all we have, don't that mean that you feels like you can take a turn in the conditions our people lives in, too?

Ellen felt a burn shoot through her core. *Ownership*, she remembered Marion saying. *Protect it fiercely.*

Carrie, she said. Rest assured, we will keep getting food to you, I swears we will. This is a chance for you to share with your neighbourhood.

Well, from what you've been sayin', we're all in the same neighbourhood. Sounds like a double standard there to me.

Sarah chimed in. Let's just all take a rest for the day. We'll all sleep on it tonight, she said. Sarah, the most peaceful of the lot. Shirley, too. Mabel and Ellen were the fiercest.

It took longer than usual for everyone to fall asleep that night. The March sisters sat around the fire, closing the door to the parlour this time around.

Now is the time, Ellen said. They're restless.

We got to redirect their angst to the cause, Mabel added.

Exactly right, my dear. Ellen nodded. We'll call another house meeting tomorrow afternoon. Make them part of the plan.

Discussions continue at the Ladies' Reading Room, with their comrades, both men and women. The March sisters had worried, on the day of the second house meeting, that everything would fall apart, that the house guests would give them up, alert the British MP of the operation. There were a few close calls. But after the meeting, after they'd been invited to join the Reading Room discussions, to become part of the plan, the flow had been restored. The fireside chats have expanded. The women take turns allowing others to get sleep and meals and warmth and proper cleanliness. They bring word to their neighbourhoods of the plan.

But Ellen worries that what Marion has taught them, to master the art of control, to operate the men with peace and reasoning while simultaneously making them believe the ideas are theirs, is losing effectiveness in this climate. While reasoning and peace have triumphed with the women from the slums, she senses there is violence percolating. Despite the March sisters' best efforts, despite their tiny bubble of sanctity, thousands of people are growing increasingly starved, malnourished, ill and angry. The air is pregnant with menace.

You knows what this is, don't ya, Ellen, says Mabel, one night in the cellar.

What is it, Mabel girl?

People are starved. Desperate. Protests, even the most well-intentioned ones, do sometimes have a way of turnin' violent.

We should be prepared, is all, is what I think she's sayin', Ellen, says Shirley.

This protest could very well turn into an eat-the-rich situation, Ellen, says Mabel.

The suffragette descendants decide at a Reading Room meeting that they'll meet at 2 p.m. at the Majestic Theatre on April 5, 1932.

We won't accept no for an answer, Ellen says. We won't leave until they respond to our request. We want those minutes investigated. They got to admit to us that those minutes were falsified, and that Squires was making secret payments to himself. Enough is enough.

Squires's finance minister had resigned on the allegations.

Two thousand people, men and women, arrive at the Majestic. Along the way, trudging along New Gower Street, away from the slums, eastbound, tromping towards Queen's Road, down towards Duckworth, up Cochrane and Military Road until they reach the Colonial Building, they've gained another fifteen hundred bodies by the time they reach the front steps.

Ladies and gentlemen! Mabel calls from the steps of the building. Please remember! We shall not defy the peaceful nature of this protest! Should you breach the peace, you will have nullified the purpose and spirit of this movement! We call for Squires to resign, we want no violence! Cheer with me! Squires resign! No violence!

Loud, dedicated, ferocious cheers echo her words.

At 3:30 p.m., the delegation is admitted, and the four sisters file inside. Ellen, Mabel, Sarah and Shirley are seated at a long table in the front of the room, facing the Chamberman, who faces the rest of the group. Outside rustles, the agitation of those awaiting the decision becoming louder.

We declare, announces the Chamberman, that Sir Richard Squires has been proven innocent in the accused falsification of chamber minutes.

NO! Ellen stands and pounds her fists on the table. NO! She shrieks it, over and over again, until her voice is raw and stinging. And then, her gut drops so hard that it's as if she feels the sepsis that roared through Marion's body, the lung infection taking over and killing all of her organs. In that moment, Ellen turns from a living soul into a zombie with a one-track mind.

She pushes past the ministers, the clergy, the men in power, fleeing the room.

Declared innocent! She shrieks at the crowd from the top step. Get the dirty goon! Don't take wooden nickels!

The crowd swoops onto the building. People clattering through doors, shattering windows, mass physical destruction.

On command, police enter with batons, swinging them left and right, not hesitating to thwack people in the face, regardless of gender or age.

The March sisters hold hands and weave through the crowd, stumbling and pushing through people, rejoining their comrades on the lawn, doing their best to help battered people up while avoiding blows to the skull themselves.

Ellen's sole mission is to spot Squires's face, his pointy nose, his white ghostly skin, his sunken, sinister eyes in that crowd. Enough. Enough of rich men taking advantage of women, of the poor, of the underprivileged. Men like Squires. Men like Eddie Duncan. Years and years of living in fear, hairs standing on end, never ever feeling safe. They must burn.

There he is! squawks a bystander close to Bannerman Road, towards Government House. He's at the side door!

Ellen tears through the crowd, her vision laser sharp on the man, a women's scarf cloaked around his head, a weak attempt at disguise, but his nose and his height give him away. Surrounded by bodyguards and members of the clergy, as if some kind of divine presence deserving protection from God.

Mabel's sense that Ellen has strayed from her proximity is strong, and she scans the crowd, squinting, until she spots a cluster of protestors, wild with wrath, charging towards the black car Squires is headed towards. There is Ellen's red beret, once Marion's. They chase the car towards Colonial Street.

Mabel follows Ellen, who has split from the crowd, a colony of ants scurrying with fierce intensity and efficiency, a single mission towards a piece of meat to envelop and carry to their nest. Ellen charges, on her own, towards Bannerman Street. She and Mabel have spoken about the tunnel that connects a certain house on Colonial to one on Bannerman. Mabel can read Ellen's mind. She catches up to Ellen, grips her hand. Here, girl. She reaches under her cloak to reveal a piece of two-by-four, full of nails. In case ya needs it.

Keeping her ear attuned to where the crowd is, Ellen stops at the house. She closes her eyes and she feels the energy, a pulsing fury. She hears the protestors pounding against the door of the house the next street over. A black taxi rolls slowly around the corner, turning from Military onto Bannerman, waiting to pick up Squires when he exits and to drive him further into cowardice. Ellen crouches close to the front door. Low, in the shadows.

BLUNDSTONE CONFUSION

The night Talia quits Blundstone Confusion, an oil tank explodes on the Southside Hills. The remaining band members sit on swings amongst a swarm of partiers in Martin's Meadow Park, the sky above the harbour bursting into a hellish orange. Crack, boom, whoosh! A smouldering black cloud lingers overhead.

The band's genesis is in the very early hours of December 16, 2007, the morning after an infamous party at 159 Gower Street. Stepping over a bumpy boot collection to get to the front door, Ash is a woman crawling in the desert, in search of water and cool air, eager for the downtown denizens who've crashed here to get the hell out and go the fuck home. Cracking open the front door, Ash squints into the Orange Crush sunrise and sticks her tongue out into the cold air, willing coffee to drip from the clouds. Holding on to the door frame, Ash hears Laura's voice from behind her. Good ol' Blundstone confusion, she mutters, and Ash laughs. Still half-drunk, she croaks, That should be the name of our band, if we ever start one.

Two months later, Meg's drums, Laura's bass and Ash's guitar from high school are moved into the basement. Meg makes herself at home on vocals. They find a groove.

Until the night they meet Talia at the Ship, playing keys with the Riffs. She'd moved downtown from Maddox Cove a year ago, away from her grandmother's house, to make a go on the St. John's music scene and start music school. Spotlight washing over her, black hair shiny and pale skin almost translucent, a dark angel about to be pulled up to heaven. Talia's onstage presence has a waiflike, ethereal, distant air about it that mismatches her heavy, focused drive. Music is her language. It's as if she's in her own separate sphere. And yet the audience is entranced. Cult-like, even. Sometimes, she'll shoot a chin lift, or a nod to the crowd, and they'll go stark raving mad.

She's deadly, Meg murmurs into Laura's ear.

Cool as *fuck*.

After the first set, Meg tugs Laura towards Talia at the bar.

Whatareyoudoing? Laura hisses. She's too good for us.

Give it up, Laura. Grow a pair.

Talia sips something clear and bubbly from a tall glass.

Hey, Meg says. That was deadly.

Oh. Talia nods at them. Hey. Thanks. She turns back to her drink but feels them hovering. Turns back. Sizes them up. Meg, in a Posie Row shift dress with multicoloured psychedelic swirls, Doc Martens nearly to the knee. Laura in a floral tunic, cinched with a wide brown belt and cowboy booties. Just like the girls in high school who Talia knew would make life easier if they were friends.

So . . . Meg starts in. We've got a band on the go. Blundstone Confusion. It's me and Laura here. Meg wags her index finger back and forth between her and Laura. And another girl, Ash. She's not here, but anyways. We're music school students. Third year. I think you're first year? We've seen you around. The profs don't really encourage us playing downtown, they think it'll distract us, but . . . we do it anyway. She shrugs. For now we're doing covers. Le Tigre,

Blondie, Neko Case, Martha and the Muffins. Stuff like that. Oh, and we fuck around with writing our own stuff sometimes.

Talia raises her eyebrows and strokes her chin. Remembers Nan's pleas to not stick to herself too much when she goes into St. John's. Let people see how sweet you are inside, she said.

We've been to a few of your shows now, Laura interjects. There's a ton of buzz about you on the scene. Dunno if you'd be into a jam sometime?

Talia leans against the bar, the grungy wood an adhesive to her elbow.

Yeah. Sure. Okay, why not? She shrugs. Forces a smile, thinking of Nan. I'd love to jam with you sometime. She sips her bubbles.

Their first gig has seven audience members.

The Peter Easton Pub: Any Nan's Living Room. Brown panel walls. Rows of trade paperbacks that smell like dank basement. French doors with brass handles: the vestibule between the bar and the living-room slash performance-space a time warp between generations. The bar belongs to the b'ys with the Labatt mesh-back caps plunked atop their noggins, arse prints indented in the bar stools. That one there, that's Bob's arse print. The one over there, that's Dave's. Pat's arse print is on the bench down that way.

The living room has become the space of the youth, the spoon collection on the wall behind the chesterfield a cosmic blast of shooting stars, housing new bands and eager fans. The Labatt hat b'ys observe the shows through the glass doors, with very minimal interest.

Blundstone Confusion destroy. In the performance space, all seven people fan their arms in the air the whole time. That was awesome, ladies, when you playin' again? says a dude with hair in his eyes, voice hoarse from bawling out all the songs, wearing a T-shirt that says *I'd rather have a bottle in front of me than a frontal lobotomy*. The Tom Waits reference makes little bubbles pop inside Talia's chest.

Blundstone Confusion continues to grow their audience. They play as many gigs as they can fit in while still maintaining their grades.

Meg has early notice that an apartment in the big house on Circular is available. Her mother lives in the basement apartment. They'll be closer to the university, and also have a jam space in the basement since Meg's mother works the night shift at the Health Sciences Centre. They've cleared it with the landlady, an artful French former ballerina with a bleeding heart.

Talia, will you move in with us? Come onnnn. Pleeease. Ash isn't ashamed to beg. Talia feels herself tense. She is comfortably uncomfortable in her tiny basement apartment on Baltimore Street. But she knows if she wants to make a go of music in this town, she has to connect with the community.

Don't forget to make friends now, my duck, Nan said, flipping Timid Talia's eggs over easy, the morning she started kindergarten. Giant orange blooms on the wallpaper, sun spilling through the big windows, the smell of buttery toast, the crackle of the CBC, the radio always on, and the sound of Nan's voice. The thought of Nan's kitchen evokes an olfactory memory, a strong nostalgic pull. *Can't I just stay here?*

Maybe this little girl wants a friend? Nan took Talia by the hand and led her over to the sandbox. Talia sat shyly next to the little girl with the side ponytail, and Nan stepped softly to the side. The girl had big fat zero hesitations bringing Talia into the game, which was to build a castle for her Rainbow Brite doll. You do that side, she said, that's the side where Starlite will have his stable. She handed Talia a triangle-shaped cup. Nan's strong, kind aura rested on Talia's shoulders and let her settle into this uncomfortable situation.

It's one week before Christmas when the girls move into Circular. Her first Christmas without Nan.

They've got no money for a moving truck, so a group of musicians form a furniture parade up Prescott. A person at each end of each mattress. Talia and Meg carry one, two sax players from the Idlers take another. Laura with a drum under each armpit. Through Rawlins Cross. Ash a walking coat stand. People marching through the streets in disguise, a group of mummers making a scene.

T'ought the Sanny Claus parade were already over! barks the man scuffing down Monkstown Road with a cart full of bottles and plastic, cackling until he coughs. Finally reaching Circular, they drag their belongings up over the fire escape–style stairs to the second-floor apartment. They have to bend their mattresses to make them fit under the sharp-angled ceilings in the tiny bedrooms. Decades ago, these would have been the servants' quarters.

Just drop your gear, guys! Ash calls from the kitchen, the tsst of a twisted bottle cap punctuating the sentence. There's beers! She takes a sip then sets it down and begins to roll a joint. The others pepper in—Laura, Meg, two sax players. Talia comes last.

Well, I guess we're family now. Ash finishes rolling the joint and joins the circle of people sitting on the kitchen floor. She sparks it up and inhales. Mommy's got a treat for ya. She raises her bottle as she passes the joint to Laura. Hands the beers around.

No thanks. Talia waves it away. She pulls a club soda from the fridge and sits cross-legged, joining them on the kitchen floor. She notes the room's frequency. The tip of her nose is cold. Her bones feel cold. Her nervous energy zaps the air.

In bed that night, her mattress feels damp from being dragged on snow, an extraterrestrial iciness. She wishes she could get up the next day and call Nan. "If Wishes Were Kisses"—Nan cranked the Perry Como tune any time it came over the scratchy kitchen radio. She'd sing it to Pop up in heaven.

On Talia's worst days, a suffocating black smoke floats around her like an unwanted, scratchy shawl. She is awake for most of the night, a scattered twenty minutes of fitful sleep here and there. All night long, she lies there, a lead weight, nose cold, eyes blinking heavily, hazily, glancing at the red numbers on her clock radio, calculating how much sleep she could still get. At one point, she swears she sees and hears the cupboard tucked beneath the sharply angled ceiling creak open. *It's just the house settling, it's just the house settling.* Swears she hears people whispering back. An auditory hallucination? An even colder breeze floats in, making the room more frigid than it was before.

She stares drowsily at the window, the street lights illuminating particles of dust floating in the air, settling her into her mattress, telling her she belongs here. She finally nods off. In her dreams, she's on the phone with Nan.

'Ow ya settlin' in, my love? Nan's voice crackles over the receiver. Are ya makin' friends?

Yeah. Friends from school.

'Ow's the new house? Where's it to again?

Circular Road. Number 74.

Oh my larsh, says Nan. Talia never understood the word *larsh.* She never asked, just figured it was an older version of gosh. Your mother lived at that house, Talia.

The dust particles sprinkle over her. What?

Yes. Delia . . . Nan's voice drifts off, goes warbly. You're so much like her . . .

Dreams are weird. The warbles of Nan's voice drown in splashing water, and next it's a low-pressure day, the sky bright white fog. Talia is on a dock. Meg, Laura, Ash. The Idlers. Her childhood piano teacher. Nan. Pop. They're all there, hugging each other goodbye. Various boats pitch dock, the friends climbing aboard one, leaving Talia alone on the dock. Don't forget the bread crumbs, Tal, Nan used to say. When you goes out on your wanders in the woods, ya gotta have something to give to the fairies. Your mother always took something with her when she went for her wanders.

Since childhood, Talia has felt the need to roam.

Eventually the night lifts into day.

Caffeination! Meg sings it operatically from the kitchen.

Talia scuffs into the kitchen, plaid shirt buttoned the wrong way, hair bordering dreadlock territory. Meg places a bright orange mug with steaming black coffee in front of her. The kitchen smells like toast and butter.

Milk? Sugar? Meg conducts the kitchen, arms sweeping in broad strokes between the coffee pot and the Becel tub, from the toaster to the cutlery drawer. She is liquid, she is brisk. She is Leonard Bernstein.

Black's good for me, Talia croaks.

So. Meg sits next to her, laying plates of toast for each of them. They hadn't managed to find a kitchen table yet, but during last night's libations, it was decided to go collect an abandoned Mary Brown's bench on the corner of George Street. The crew marched it across Water Street, up Prescott, down Monkstown, past Winterholme and finally to Circular.

Talia and Meg sit, carefully. The bench isn't fully fastened to the wall yet and threatens to slide away. Sitting there is a gamble. Brown plastic placemats from Meg's parents' house between them, little fork marks in the plastic from when she and her sisters were kids—

markers of a completely different childhood than Talia experienced, one full of noise and people and bustle.

How'd you sleep? Meg pops a brand-new jar of Cheez Whiz and dives her knife into the untouched goo.

Not bad, Talia shrugs, thinking about the pack of Dramamine she'd dug into and how she'd pondered tossing the whole pack down her throat.

It's weird adjusting to a new place, for sure. How does your room feel?

Cold. She answers quickly, a chill shivering down her spine. I had weird dreams.

Meg shimmies half an inch closer to Talia. The late night didn't help, I'm sure. Sorry, Talia, if we kept you awake. I think this place will start to warm up soon. We'll make it cozy. She sips her coffee. Shakes her head. I miss the coffee in Montreal, she says. I stayed with my cousin in Montreal for two months last summer, at her dorm at U of M. I love it there. Meg stares dreamily towards the ceiling. It's just so . . . romantic. Artful. I want to live there someday.

I've never been, Talia says, feeling like she's still dreaming.

That's okay, you can move there with me. We'll meet some gorgeous men, live whole new lives. Write songs. Play at Jazz Fest. Have amazing sex. Smoke cigarettes.

Eat croissants instead of Cheez Whiz?

Ha! Yeah, really.

So . . . I think my mom might've lived in this house a long time ago. Talia wraps her hands around her orange mug to warm them.

Meg's eyes widen and Talia notes the one speckle of hazel inside her green iris. What?! Shut the front door.

Yeah. I remember my nan telling me that Mom lived in town when she was in university, in a big old mansion. Mom was a hippy and lived in the house with a bunch of her friends back in the '70s. My nan's brother was the owner and caretaker.

And this is the house?

I can't be sure about that, but last night I dreamed I was on the phone with Nan, and she told me. I remember Nan saying that Mom told her it felt spooky in the house sometimes.

Wild. Meg sips her coffee. Crunches her Cheez Whiz toast. Chews. Swallows. Just fucking *wild.* She shakes her head, remembering all the moments she spent in the driveway playing hopscotch, trekking around the neighbourhood, the time when that guy Joe lived with her and her mom for a while . . . the wildness of time, of place, recycling themselves.

Laura appears, scuffing into the kitchen. She seems grumpy in the mornings. Talia relates.

Laura, Meg says, toast crumbs falling on her pyjama top. Talia's mom lived here once.

Humph, Laura says, heading straight for the coffee pot.

Talia. Meg's voice is gentle. Do you mind if I ask what happened to your mom? I know you were raised by your nan and pop.

Talia tenses. I've got a practice room booked for ten, she says. Sorry.

Oh. Meg shimmies off the bench to let Talia up. Sorry, Talia, I didn't mean to . . .

No, it's okay. Tell you later. She hurries towards her room to change. She wants to share. She trusts Meg. She is drawn to her warmth. She feels like she always felt in Nan's kitchen. Safe. Now even more so, with the knowledge that they both have a historical, familial connection to this house. The walk to the music building is filled with notes of a bright future.

By the time she closes the door to the practice room, her mind has travelled back in time. Nan's funeral. The last walk Pop took in the woods. Half of the time, Pop would be dressing up in women's clothes, dancing around the house, trying to make Talia laugh. The other half, he was off by himself, for hours, returning with a tear-stained face and reeking of Famous Newfoundland Screech Rum. Grief comes out of nowhere sometimes.

With just enough space for her and the piano, the practice pod is a fortress of solitude. A place where her thoughts can be free enough and safe enough to swirl into the mesosphere with the notes she produces. She sits on the bench and unfolds the music book before her. Wriggles until her sitting bones plant themselves into the bench. Rests her fingertips gently on the keys. The smooth ebony and ivory pull her back in time, to the upright Steinway in Nan's living room. Nan, who saved a quarter from each of her pension cheques for a year to buy it. Paid for Talia's lessons. Never missed a recital.

Talia was only a baby when her mother died. Delia was a free spirit, Nan had told her. Her soul was beautiful, curious, a field of wildflowers, said Nan. But she was a fairy, and fairies are into some bad things, Nan told her.

Talia's fingertips pulse as they tap and press down on the smooth surface of the keys, as if her blood is seeping beyond her skin, into the wood, her veins expanding into the insides of the piano. Her fingers glide and press, effortlessly. Crescendo, decrescendo. Conjuring memories of her grandfather, immersed in his fiddle or his accordion. Sometimes he cried while he played. Dragging the bow across the strings. Pressing the accordion keys, expanding and compressing the bellows, apart and together and apart again, decrescendo, crescendo, releasing melancholy melodies into the atmosphere.

It had been three days since Pop returned from his final walk. Talia was fifteen. Nan paced the floor of her sunshine kitchen. It's that devil's drink, she said. For the love of Jesus, Talia, don't ever touch that poison. It'll kill ya. Sensitive souls, like your grandfather and you . . . The fairies, they smells it and they can't resist it.

Pop was a seventh son of a seventh son. The seventh male child born in an unbroken line with no female siblings born between, and to a father who himself was the seventh male in an unbroken line. Many people in the Cove came to Pop with their ailments, begging him to cure them. Nan believed he carried this burden heavily. He could not separate their pain from his own. *Rather have a bottle in front of me than a frontal lobotomy . . .*

Her syncopation flicks to staccato, and Talia lifts her eyes open like she's going in for the kill. Bores her gaze into the keyboard. Pizzicato. Frantic. Angry. Jabbing stabbing. Each note shocks her with a painful memory. She glares so hard at the keys that soon she is feeling and seeing below the white and black, into the wood grains, underneath the lid of the baby grand. Stuck in the strings, full throttle, ducking from the plunking keys, diving to stay alive.

Sometimes Talia takes the long way home. Walks past Circular, up to Signal Hill. Stands and looks at the ocean in the dark. It's a long walk. But being folded into the woods, next to the crashing waves, gives her a strange comfort. A connection to Pop maybe, or her mother—wherever they are.

That evening, when she approaches the crescent-shaped driveway, the landlady is putting garbage in a bin.

Bonsoir, mademoiselle! She waves.

Talia waves back.

The woman strolls towards her. Have you a moment?

Talia waits there.

We did not meet when your friend signed the lease. The woman extends her hand. I am Élodie.

Talia takes the woman's small, soft hand in her own.

I hear you are musicians? You play piano?

Yes, I do.

Classical, I assume? If you are in music school?

Yeah. But I love to rock, too. I sing, too.

Well . . . The woman smiles. I have a piano in the main house, should you ever need to use it. I know the desire to connect to your art. You need it to *live*, oui?

Yes. Talia looks at the pavement.

Wings flap and a crow caws directly above Élodie's shoulder, startling Talia.

Ah. Don't mind Brandon Lee. He hangs around sometimes. Stands guard, I suppose.

I wish the rest of us could tune in to your frequency, Talia, says Laura after their last jam before the Martin's Meadow Park show. It'll be their last show of the summer before the fall semester starts.

Talia feels a twinge of jealousy from Laura, in general.

We'll never be on Tal's frequency, Laura, Ash says. That's why she's in the band. She gives us this, like, mystical quality. People are fuckin' gaga over her. Like, in a trance. Ash opens her eyes wide and drops her mouth open and hangs her tongue out and they all laugh.

Yeah, Meg says, Talia's like our Cherie Currie. Our troublemaker. She winks at Talia. She's thought about asking Talia if she's okay so many times, but never got the guts.

The night of the show is sweaty and humid in the park across from South Side Hills. They've been building to it all year. Ash made a

Facebook account so she could promote it for free, and over two hundred people clicked that they were "Going."

People spill into the park. A cacophony of cackles and coughs, tinkles of clinking bottles, the *sspht* of caps popping off, kicked and pressed into the gravel for some kid in the sandbox to find the next day. Inhalations and coughs, twirls of burning weed smoke curling into the sky.

Laura plunks a bass string hard to get things on the go. Meg spills off a drum riff. Ash shrieks, Are you ready people??

They tear into the set. The Runaways. Kate Bush. PJ Harvey. Smashing Pumpkins, *Mellon Collie and the Infinite Sadness*. Tonight, tonight. The crowd gets increasingly riled. Losing their minds, drunk high, givin' 'er. Drive it home so hard they dig a grave. They finish the show, the gibbous moon silver against the night sky.

When the music ends and the drinking takes over, it's easy for Talia to slink away undetected, weaving silently through the crowd towards the steps to exit the park. She pounds the downtown streets. Panting, gasping for nature.

Forehead clammy, she reaches the base of Signal Hill. Climbs, off-trail, through brambles, skin scratched. Bugs buzz. Pointy nose. Squinting, menacing eyes. Spiky features, from the branches. Then . . . moosh. Into a boggy pile of guck. Cackling all around her, coming from the black night air, her skin full of pricks and pins. Through the twigs and the darkness, she sees that it's fairies, biting at her arms and legs and face. She's been dreaming of them for weeks. Climbing all over her. Earlobes. Up in her nose. On the back of her neck. Her armpits, elbows, all over. Crawling. Threatening.

She finds a spot on a large, smooth boulder. Pats her pockets for bread. Plants herself there, on the rock, mesmerized until—over on the Southside Hills—an explosion. She tosses crumbs into the twigs and shadows.

Oh just fuck off, she says. All falls silent, but for the *cshhht* of the smoke and the sirens in the distance.

Meg squints through the crowd, panic rising. Where's Talia?

She looks across the harbour. Scans the dark coastline. From the dark ashes, she swears she sees her, rising.

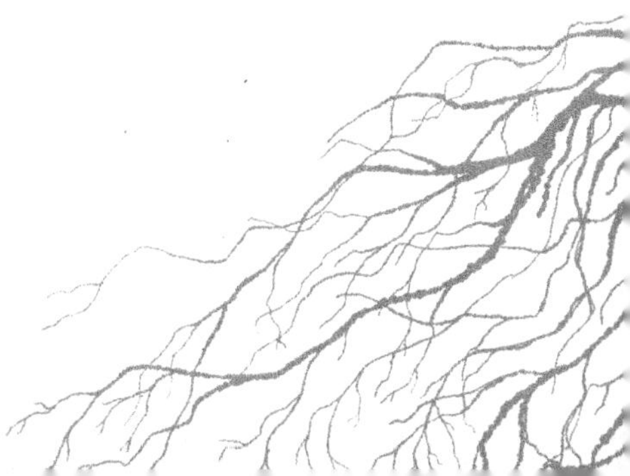

TRIPTYCH

The melancholy cello of the 1965 Jacqueline du Pré recording crackled from the gramophone Élodie bought at Rosewood Antique Shop. The first of many, many purchases after the deed on The House had gone through.

Arms swooped overhead, forming an invisible and desperately desired rainbow, face skyward, scrunched in agony before quickly lurching her body forward, lifeless, arms dangling, head drooping, bouncing there, sorrow dripping from her skull, red like blood, salty like tears. Each legato note drew anguish which she then hurled from her body by tossing an arm or swooping her torso or pounding a fist. Reckless contortions, twists, unnatural bends. The antiballet. The kind of dance she would only do while alone, trying desperately to eject the pain trapped in her tiny frame, occupying the great expanse of the house with profound loneliness.

I watched from my perch at the top of the curly staircase. My favourite place when I'm inside. Hesitant to even breathe, or flutter a feather, as quiet as a mouse, fearful of breaking the spell she has cast. And yet . . . I believe that she *wants* me spying on her. She likes knowing I am there. *She* relies on *me*.

I arrived here in this house right after Otto, Élodie's husband, left. I'd fallen from my nest and cracked a leg. Elle found me there, lying in a cracked pile, and her expression melted from placid to aggrieved, as if she felt my pain.

Mon dieu! she'd exclaimed, ever so gently scooping me up and cradling me in her forearm and hand. From first touch, her grief, embedded so deep that she eternally ached, percolated into my own blood. As she lifted me, a glimmer flashed and fell into the bush. I couldn't tell if it was real or just a sunny sparkle bouncing off a shiny object, but there wasn't any time to explore it before I was carried inside the house, which brimmed with nearly as much life as the outdoors. Plants crawled the walls. Felines, slinking under the tables, weaving around chair legs, creeping around the corners of doorways.

We must fix you up, you poor thing.

Inside, her daughter, a young teenager, sat at the kitchen table.

What the fuck is *that*? Maman, not another animal, *please*!

Shhh, come now, Louise, watch your language, s'il te plaît! This poor crow is in pain! He is a living creature, just as we are. We must *nurture* him.

The girl rolled her eyes. There are already, like, twelve animals living in this house, said Louise. You are not bringing another one in here. It's disgusting.

Come now, my Lulu. Votre coeur. Don't forget it. Would you not want someone to heal you if you broke your leg falling from a tree?

A cat hissed under the table.

A bird in a house full of cats, scoffed Lulu, that'll end well.

Shh, Oscar. Elle spoke softly. Go do what cats do. Chase mice. Climb the curtains. Lick your fur. Lulu, go get me the Popsicle sticks, please.

Fucking ridiculous, the girl murmured, shoving her chair backwards, storming towards The Cabinet of Random Items. String. Paper clips. A pincushion. A Gaudi key ring from Barcelona. A broken magnet from Prague. A miniature Eiffel Tower.

She tossed a fistful of Popsicle sticks onto the table and they scattered.

Merci, ma fille. Oblivious to Lulu's anger, or pretending to be (I honestly couldn't tell which it was), she smiled at her daughter, who glowered in return. The woman seemed to float around in her own sphere, separate from the one the rest of us existed in. A haze, different colours at different times, surrounded her.

Ever-so-delicately, she flanked my leg with Popsicle sticks and wrapped white tape around it. She carried me into the living room. The fabric on the couch and the drapes exploded with bursts of red and pink roses and tropical green monstera leaves. The velvet and silk wallpaper, crawling with tiny vines, shimmering, tempted me to peel it off the walls and present it as a gift.

She perched me on the piano, next to the couch, and pulled the French doors closed so the cats wouldn't get me. There, she said. Stay here as long as you like. Pay no attention to the grumpy girl in the kitchen. She misses her friends in Europe. She misses her father. She does not yet realize that anger is but a jacket for sadness.

Elle's eyes sparkled with tears. Her shoulders slumped forward, and she dropped her head into her hand and let the tears drop, her pain seeping into my feathers. I wished I could fly away with it.

As my leg healed, Elle brought me for daily visits to the garden. Fed me crunched-up cornflakes and squished-up berries. French fries and croissant flakes and jam.

That's still here? Louise said, after a month. Don't you think he should be off in the wild again?

Well, I bring him outside every day, but every day he stays. So. She shrugged. If he wants to stay? He stays. I think we should name him. Otto.

We are *not* naming him after Papa. Are you actually insane?

As I flapped around in the tree, Elle sank down onto the porch swing. Oh, she said. I did not even realize . . .

She trailed off, gazing off towards the river.

You did not realize? How could you not realize? Lulu's arms were crossed, but as she continued to frown at her mother, her stern brow eventually softened into something that resembled pity. Her mother had drifted into that dark place again, that place of silence and deathly lonesomeness. Elle only stared at the trees, her hands twisting in agitation in her lap. Lulu huffed and rolled her eyes to the sky. Dropped her arms and plunked herself down next to her mother on the swing.

Why don't we call him Brandon Lee? That seems like a name for a tough old bird. She nudged her mother.

Elle laid her head on her daughter's shoulder. Brandon Lee? Okay. She sniffed. Brandon Lee it shall be.

When she was sure her maman was not around, Louise sometimes spoke to herself. Or, perhaps, as time went on, as she got used to me. Well, maybe she was speaking to me.

The way she still loves Papa makes me *sick*, she spat. Asshole. Left us cold. No warning. Now everything is *shit*.

She sat at her desk and scratched in her sketchbook, stabbing the paper with each dotting of an *i* and crossing of a *t*:

<u>*You:*</u>
You don't think I notice you:
Staying attuned to "opportunities."
These days it's the student with the wild and curly hair.

This is Sasha, you introduced her, in the Avalon Mall.
A twinkle in your eye at the shiny new thing.

Noticing my mother's forehead wrinkles,
Her crow's feet.
Hopelessly devoted to you.
Ignoring your secret desire for more.
Because she believes in your devotion to her.

You crave the chemical flutter of newness;
It hovers around you, bores into you,
an eternal temptation.
Now we live in a thick, grey haze.
It feels like this is just how life is now, forever.
Happiness is just some storybook crock of shit that doesn't exist anymore.

The poor girl threw the pen across the room and slunk onto the floor and wept. Dragged herself up onto her bed and screeched into a pillow until she was too tired to cry anymore, drifting into a deep and tortured slumber.

I watched Elle in a reclusive state, glass after glass, bottle after bottle of vodka and then squirrelling the stash away in places she thought no one saw. (Lulu saw.) I made my perch on the stairs and filled the large and lonely vastness with my caws.

Will you shut UP! Lulu shrieked. God! It feels so creepy in here! She'd storm up the stairs and slam her bedroom door. I bled black blood for her.

I flew to her bedroom each night, to keep her company, while she did homework. Sometimes she'd open her door and let me in. If not, I'd just wait outside the door, trusting that she knew I was there.

Maman barely notices I'm here, she said to me one night, while I perched on her windowsill. She drinks constantly, Lulu continued. I can't tell if she thinks I don't know, or if she just doesn't care that I know and does it anyway, or if she's just that out of it. It's like she's performing her own life, in a soap opera or ballet. The tragic prima ballerina, heartbroken and dejected. No one wants her. Like she's starring in *Whatever Happened to Baby Jane?* or *Sunset Boulevard* or some shit. Except it's not even like I'm in the audience. Like I'm a ghost. And she's a ghost.

Lulu scrawled viciously in her notebooks. Highlighted ferociously. It was her senior year, and she didn't care about university. She only wanted to get into dance school. To leave Newfoundland.

She wrote in her diary. Angry scrawls that I could not read, being a crow and all.

I can't stay here in this depressing place for one second after high school. Fuck this greyness. I can't stand to look at her most of the time. She's skin and bones. Completely obsessed with herself. Doesn't even notice how I'm doing. Any time she shows me affection, I feel like that's an act too. I will never be like her. I will be strong. I will get out of here, and I will never come back.

I watched Lulu practice in the studio in the basement. Her costumes were black, navy, metallic. Her movements stiff. Rigid. Cutting. Slicing. More like her mother than she'd ever concede. They both needed dance to extract their pain.

Lulu had not seen the dance I had seen, in private, when Elle thought no one was watching. When she let herself move freely. I know her affection for Lulu could not be more real. I felt it from her heart in my own heart. Whenever Elle attempted to show love, her daughter would recoil as if she'd been scalded. Did she ever consider how that would feel? I sometimes worried she'd lost all empathy for her mother.

But Elle continued to teach ballet to the little girls of St. John's. The little darlings arrived at the front door, lifting the giant iron door knocker with their tiny hands and birdlike bones, dropping it, not waiting for someone to answer before scurrying inside, giggling and gleeful. Scampering about, looking for the cats and the dog and the frog. I usually liked to stay out of the way, perched in my usual place at the top of the stairs. I'd watch the little girls enter the house, their reflections in the mirror at the bottom of the stairs, and the look of delight on Élodie's face as she entered the foyer to greet them.

Now, my little darlings! Downstairs! Quickly! She'd snap her fingers and clap her hands and lead them towards the back of the house, ducklings following their mother, towards the stairs that lead to the studio in the basement. Sometimes, begrudgingly at first, Lulu assisted. It was the one time I witnessed mother and daughter in harmony. They weren't talking to each other, they were parallel playing. It brought Lulu joy, as well, to help shape the little dancers.

The way they all line up, just as they're told, Lulu said in her room one night, bending their knees, reaching their arms above, stretching tall, leaning from side to side, lilting to the music . . . She trailed off, transported to a different time. Reminds me of when I was little, I guess.

Go tell your mother, I wanted to say to her. This is a connection! But it only came out as a cuh-caw. I watched her write, and imagined what it might say:

I do wish, sometimes, that we were more like we were when I was little. Watching the little girls with her, and how happy they make her, and how sad I make her . . . Dancing saves us. I wish I had more strength to be nicer to her. I wish I knew how to let go of the rage I always feel. I resent her for being so pathetic. I want her to move on, be strong. Sometimes I blast empowering songs from my bedroom, hoping something will seep in. I even stooped to Spice Girls once. Dammit, that song is catchy. Aretha Franklin. Helen Reddy. But I guess Maman isn't ready yet. Still nothing from Papa. Coward. I thought I was his world.

When others were in the house, Lulu's aura turned from grey-blue to lavender. She morphed from low-lying, suffocating, pregnant-with-rain cumulonimbus clouds to the more floating and free altocumulus clouds. I didn't feel the same urge to caw and fill up empty, sad space. After a while, during those times, I often left the house. Floated outside, above the garden, sailing farther up, perching on the chimney top to scan the neighbourhood. What other pain and joy and anger and peace existed under those many roofs? I tilt my head towards the wispy, detached cirrus clouds.

It was Melanie, the mother of one of the little ballerinas, who suggested that Élodie host some of the singers who would be visiting for Festival 500—an international choral festival being presented in St. John's as part of the anniversary of John Cabot's supposed discovery of Newfoundland and Labrador.

There are choirs from countries all over the world, I overheard the woman explaining one Saturday, her daughter and another little girl running circles around her waist. There's a committee meeting next week if you'd like to come. You can meet Doreen Day, the director of the festival. She conceptualized it and she is a delight. And you've got all of this *gorgeous* space. I know it's an ordeal having people stay with you, so no pressure, but if you wanted to think about it . . .

I will think about it, oui.

Élodie perked up, I could see it from my perch. Her shoulders straightened. Her chin lifted. So did the corners of her mouth.

Please, let me know if you have questions. Call me any time! The woman shepherded the squealing little girls out of the house. Stop slapping each other! she said as she closed the door behind her.

When the last of the students had left that day, I remained in my place, just listening. Elle was in the parlour. I heard the fine crystal decanter pouring vodka into a glass. Moments later, I smelled the cigarette smoke.

I'd been a background player on the set of this scene many times in the past:

Sitting on the chesterfield in the bay window of the parlour, or sometimes on the piano bench, plants surrounding her—giant ferns begging to burst through the window, an umbrella plant, ivy crawling up the walls, curling around the curtain rod—she just gazed out the window. Her big brown eyes, framed with thick black eyeliner drawn in the dramatic cat eyes of the 1970s, held a wide vacancy, stared far into space as if she was somewhere else. Smoking. Sipping. Staring. Sobbing. Sometimes for hours, a symphony of inhales and exhales and gulps and pours and snivels and groans and tears. I had plucked a cigarette or two from the cushions in my beak, leaving a burn hole behind.

I brought her gifts. Shiny things. I knew she liked antiques. One day, around the rose bush, I fished out a gold ring. The glimmer I'd thought was an illusion on the day she found me. When I laid it in front of her, she collapsed.

I thought I'd lost it forever, she wept, shoving it onto her wedding-ring finger. I cannot thank you enough. She crawled upstairs to her bed. Lay in the fetal position, face in her pillow, until she cried herself to sleep.

Why did you bring her that thing? Lulu barked at me when I visited her that night. It's only a reminder of her heartbreak. You shouldn't have brought that here. And she shooed me out of her room and slammed the door.

Later that evening, after Melanie has left the house with her little ballerinas, I watch Elle dance to Jacqueline du Pré. Something feels different this time. She drops the needle on the record. She sways with the cello, simple knee bends from side to side, her arms rising skyward, moving without any control, as if in a trance. It's the first time I've seen her move this way. She moves the way Lulu moves when she dances. With abandon. Total freedom. Her eyes look bright. She smiles. She also sobs. She heaves herself through the music, each note, each string extracting something from her body, releasing it into the air to be carried away. Finally, when the record ends, she crawls back to the chesterfield and falls into a deep sleep. I stay by her side, perched on the plant stand, until she wakes the next morning. She rises, she scuffs to the kitchen. Puts on the kettle. Pads up the stairs, returning moments later, makeup washed away, a fresh housecoat. She makes coffee. Pushes the toast down and, mixed with the smell of coffee, it fills the kitchen with homeyness. Picks up the phone. Dials. Waits.

Ah, bonjour, Melanie? This is Élodie. Oui, yes. I have decided, I will come to the committee meeting after all. Is there something I can bring?

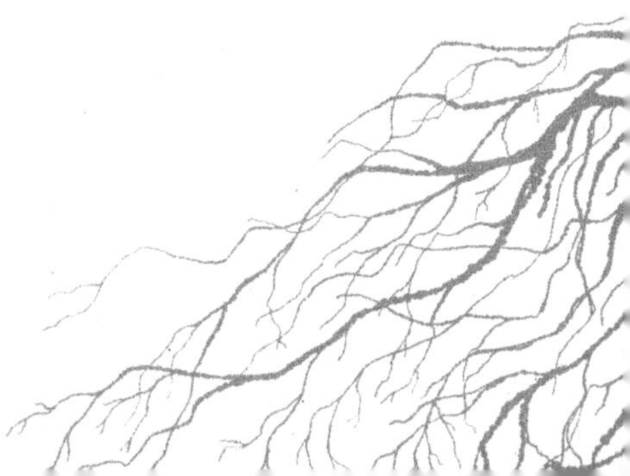

VERISIMILITUDE

The skyscrapers loom above me. Yet I am safe, floating in my H_2O cocoon, on the roof of the Hotel Bonaventure. The chlorine steam is a warm, olfactory shawl around my shoulders, protecting me from the vehicle beeps and barmps on the Montreal streets below. Even farther below, the subway swooshes. My skull tilts backwards so my ears dip just below the water's surface. The world muffles: an auditory anamorphosis. The lapping waves lull me away from the surrounding drinking-laughing-splashing pool people, into a separate dimension.

I pull myself out of the pool to recline in a lounge chair by the pool, getting crispy in the sun and woozy on dirty martinis. I watch my red toenails wiggle. Vivaldi in my earbuds, turquoise water sparkling, my thoughts bake into my body before my eyelids droop closed. Just before drifting into sunny slumber, I sense Gavin's feet padding around on the pool deck. He sets his drink on the table between us. Serene and smitten, I inhale the scent of his skin, sunscreen and chlorine, our molecules interconnecting within our own personal biosphere. Heavy eyelids half lift to a tickle on my big toe: a baby dragonfly, seemingly slow-blinking its long eyelashes at me for several moments before deep sleep cloaks my mind. This is exactly what I imagined living here would be like when I dreamed of it in my twenties.

But the next day, Sunday, the train ride back to our apartment after shopping and lunch, feels solemn.

Lately, Gavin floats between affectionate, flirty, connected—forging intense eye contact, caressing my hair, running his long fingers down my back, along my bottom—and disconnected and vacant. Barely saying a word, shrinking away from touch, sitting on his own, he fingers a percussion instrument on his knees.

On the Friday night, we had smoked a giant joint, rolled around in the fresh hotel sheets, drained every mini from the bar, ordered Reuben sandwiches and passed out.

Saturday morning, lounged by the pool, drank coffee and smoothies. His fingers stroked my fingers and my fingers stroked his fingers and the more we get together, the happier we'll feel. A tingle between my legs. I alight from within, surging a pulsing red-and-pink glow, emanating a joy I've never felt before.

Until he turns to cold wax.

Then, I am enveloped in darkness. Anchorless, without gravity, looking down at my own body, wondering what I did wrong.

Before our weekend away, back in the orchestra pit, I slide a chunk of wax along the horsehair. Tighten my bow. Pling, tune the strings. Gavin in his usual chair, his viola shining under the hot spotlights from the rigorous polishing he gave it last night.

I tried to connect. Are you oka—

Yeah. He didn't look up.

It's one of the four horsemen of relationships, you know. My friend Cathy, a psych student at McGill, is my confidante. Stonewalling. When Gavin refuses to talk to you like that? It's stonewalling. It leaves you feeling abandoned, so he's triggering your abandonment wounds, too. I know you love him, but Meg, that is toxic. And these swings in his personality worry me. Sorry. I know you don't want to hear this.

Cathy is smart, has my best interests at heart. But . . . everyone has personality fluctuations. Everyone has moods. She's not there when Gavin cooks spaghetti or buys flowers for our crappy Ikea table. When he cradles the back of my head in his palm and holds my head between his poet's fingers and kisses me longingly. Cathy doesn't see that he's just a wanderer, drifting along the musical staff of life, forever scanning the sidelines and the horizon for the next interesting venture. Curious about the world and everything in it. That's all. He has a poet's heart. Needs time to ponder. I understand that. I am enamoured by it.

It's okay for us to have space sometimes, I reply to Cathy. It's healthy, actually.

I mindfully swallow my coffee, pretending I don't notice Cathy's eyeballs rocketing skyward.

The end-of-season party always happens at the conductor's house in the Plateau. This year, it happens to fall on the June full moon, the Strawberry Moon. Hot, muggy. Girls in floral spaghetti-strap dresses, boys in their button-down linen. Prosecco flows like natural spring water, almost straight into the mouths of the nymphs who dance free around it.

Our rehearsal schedule is rigorous. Musicians are given a breathalyzer each morning. If someone blows above zero point five per cent, they're sent away. If it happens once more, they're kicked out of the orchestra. We are expected to hyperfocus at every millisecond. Our playing must be immaculate by performance night.

But there are no rules at the end-of-season party.

I am shocked when Gavin is sent home. We shared half a bottle of wine last night, but just one glass each before dinner. I went to bed before Gavin. Usually he's the one to remind *me* to stop drinking. It didn't occur to me that he would have another glass.

Gavin, is there something going on? I ask him that evening. He sits on the edge of the bed. Positions his long chin into his long fingers and stares straight ahead. And so, I keep staring at *him*. I don't know what else to do. Two of us, frozen, our molecules floating around each other but never touching, in this tiny, rigid ecosphere. I feel like, without even touching me, he is pushing me away, willing me way into the mesosphere.

Gavin, can you hear me? I try again. I understand how you feel right now. I feel it sometimes too.

Gavin lowers his face into his fingers and closes his eyes and rubs his head for several minutes, soothing himself. I inch gently towards him and sit on the mattress. His body stiffens. An invisible shield has been slammed down between us. I'm afraid to touch him, but decide the risk is worth it. If I can just break through . . . I lay one finger on his shoulder and he jolts away. My chest sears. I feel heavy on the bed.

When I was a little girl, sometimes I'd get fever dreams. My fingers felt huge, but my body felt tiny. I would float from my body and see myself from above, tiny on a massive bed, but then giant on a tiny bed. The image and accompanying sensation would waver like that, back and forth, back and forth, big and then small.

I am not really here, I remember thinking.

I guess I'll go for a walk, I squeak out, my voice barely above a whisper. It takes everything in me to stand up from the bed, my depressive angst magnetizing me into the mattress. But I get up.

The coffee is already hot and poured when I awake on the couch the next morning. Gavin squeezes fresh orange juice.

You were out cold. He kisses the top of my head and lightly scratches my head with his fingertips.

Inside, I am snarled into knots of barbed wire. I don't trust this. But I allow myself to lean my cheek into his palm for a moment. The skin-to-skin connection and affection feel nice.

I hear Cathy's voice in my mind. It's love-bombing, she tells me.

He didn't used to be this divergent. He'd been playing with the orchestra for a year before I was accepted. There was just one violinist and one violist separating our chairs. As I took my instrument from the case on that first day of rehearsal, our glances locked on each other for a moment that seemed to stretch long enough that I felt myself bloom. The twinkle in his eye was infectious, and when I returned his smile, his got larger, and I felt that he was blooming inside, too. We spent many evenings together, listening to records. Miles Davis. The Beatles. Steve Reich.

All Beatles songs are in the key of C major, he insisted.

"Eleanor Rigby" isn't, I teased.

It sounds like it isn't, he countered, but it actually is.

No. It's one hundred per cent in E minor.

Well, it opens with a C major vocal harmony though.

That doesn't make it C major. He stiffened at my push back. The moment stands out in my memory as the first of many moments like that to follow.

I move through the days wondering which version of him I'll get, swooping between peace and defensiveness, bracing myself for the next time I'm left in silence.

The last performance of the year began with a feeling of dissonance. Tumultuousness. By the third movement, things had evened out, synchronicities realigned, grooves found. The program finished with a standing ovation.

At the party, I bite into the flesh of a juicy strawberry, pretending I'm not observing Gavin seeding himself throughout the crowded space. His gaze weaves throughout the room as he speaks to one particular woman for quite some time. The strawberry feels mealy in my mouth as I chew. In between his twinkling smiles that deep-dive into her pupils, his gaze swims to see where I am and if I'm watching. Strategically placed behind a tall percussionist, I remain across the room, across the universe, shifting my gaze between the percussionist and Gavin. When I think about it, even during the good times, there was always only one eye on me. The other one was always wandering. If he was a tempo, he'd be rubato: speeding up, slowing down, never consistent. Atonal. Indecipherable.

I wish Cathy was here. You deserve so much more than that, Meg, she'd say.

Before the party, we'd met for an espresso.

Today in my lit class, we talked about verisimilitude, I told her. Basically, it means questioning the rules of reality. I stared at a photo of cats drinking coffee that hung on the wall across from our table.

That's a term in the psych world too, Cathy said. The concept is based on intuition that a theory is closer to the truth when the theory allows us to make fewer false predictions. Belief versus progress kind of thing.

Cats drinking coffee. Like that could happen.

Don't forget your intuition, Megsy.

Gavin isn't in my eye line anymore.

Something clicks inside my body. I become hyperfocused. My heart turns electric. Adrenaline spikes and I dart my eyes around the room, and when I don't find him, I skirt through the crowd, warp speed, until I reach the foot of the winding staircase in the foyer of the giant house. Gavin's elbows rest on the banister, leaning forward, smiling at the girl. She's standing a few steps below him, on the floor, fawning, stars in her eyes.

I march right up to them.

Hey! I extend my hand to her. I'm Meg. Gavin's girlfriend. Second violin.

A whoosh of realization washes over her face, and I can read her thoughts, instantly and precisely. She simply raises her hands in the air, steps backwards and dissolves into the people.

Um, what's that about? Gavin acts like I'm acting crazy. And I feel like I might be, but in an empowered, fuck-this-shit sort of way.

What is real? Is what Gavin and I have even real? Perhaps Gavin is not who I think he is or who I want him to be.

I don't like how you're acting, I tell him.

His expression softens, and he touches my shoulder. He does care about me, is the thing. As much as he has the capacity to care, he cares. Wanna just go for a ride? He flicks his glance towards the door. Bike's outside, he says.

I soften, just slightly, but the rigidity in my body remains strong.

Okay, I say. On Gavin's motorcycle, gliding around the roads, curving sharp corners, puts us into a realm of togetherness where words don't exist. I just have to clasp my arms around his waist and hug myself into him and we are stuck together, zipping through life, our molecules entwined and dancing together.

Regardless of the future, I know I will always have access to love for Gavin.

We'll head to Mount Royal? Usual route?

I nod my head and feel myself relax, just a smidge. We clip our helmets on, and I hoist my leg over the back seat and assume my regular position behind him. He revs the engine. We start moving and time means nothing. Other people mean nothing.

Here is everything.

Usually on the bike, as we drive, the angst of my world cracks away from my body and shatters on the pavement behind me.

But tonight, the fear escalates the faster we go. Gavin's energy is orange and red, and it surges into my body as he pushes harder on the accelerator.

Gavin! I yell.

He doesn't hear me. Faster.

Gavin! I scream. Gavin! I shriek.

Almost at the top of Mount Royal, in the woods, we hit a sharp curve. Skid violently on loose gravel. The back of the motorcycle swerves back and forth. I vibrate in terror, gripping my fingers into his body, holding on for dear life, until finally I cannot hold on to this man, this body, this semblance of a reality any longer, and I release and fly off the back of the bike, into the atmosphere. Branches scrape my side and I land on my back and I look up at the trees high above me, the stars in the black sky. Exhaust fumes. Then . . . nothing.

The dragonfly toe-tickle flutters to between my legs. Gavin and I are wrapped in a hot, thick sleeping bag. We grind and wind together. I groan, I release, the euphoric ex-thrill-eration quick-eclipsed by terror. Gavin's sunscreen-chlorine heat turns sludgy and cold, smelling and feeling like wet leaves and soil. I am suffocated and it's near impossible to draw a breath. I gasp awake, the hot sun singeing my forehead and nose, my mouth hot, my saliva thick as blood.

The sun melts into a glaring examination light in a hospital. The morphine they've been giving me causes the most intense dreams.

A man in a white coat hovers above me.

Megan? Can you hear me? Can you blink twice for yes?

I blink twice.

Do you remember why you're here? Blink twice for yes.

I blink twice.

They'd told me I have pseudocoma, also called locked-in syndrome, the result of severe head trauma experienced during the accident. Motor functions unlikely to ever return. However, there are new interfaces where implants can allow computers to read my thoughts.

Like light trail photography, my memory zooms backwards to when I was a child and Joe was brought to the hospital, given a less morbid diagnosis. I wish I had his diagnosis now. I remember feeling so sorry for Joe at the time, pitying him. There was a time when I could think for myself and didn't need a computer to read my thoughts.

I sink my head back into the Hotel Bonaventure pool.

There are realms. Humans, spectres—from the present or past—coexist within the same sphere. The present is forever haunted, or comforted, by the past.

Energies travel, between beings, through time and space. Somewhere, our molecules still occupy the same atmosphere, melding together in harmony, dissonance left in the dust.

Somewhere, I have a new lover. A better lover. A real lover. Somewhere, Cathy and I are elderly ladies on our front veranda in rocking chairs, staring at the clouds.

Somewhere, I am still an infant, a multiverse waiting for me at every horizon.

There, Gavin and I sip cocktails at the Hotel Bonaventure.

Here, I am back in my childhood home, in St. John's, on Circular Road, in the same bed I lay in when giant syndrome set in. The same bed I lay in when I thought about what would happen to Joe. My mother visits me several times daily, bringing me trays of ice chips and blueberries, doing her best to woo me back to the womb and deliver me into a new life.

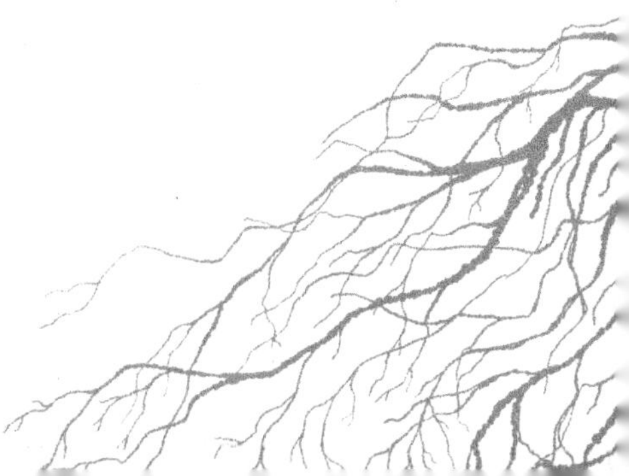

ANATOMY OF A WAVE

The strawberry patch is packed with people picking the bugs' breakfast.

June holds Murl's arm, the old woman's obesity dragging June's right shoulder downwards, towards the earth and soil. In the backwards trajectory of June's memory, berry picking was a part of every single summer. A day around the bay for blueberries, their townie backyard for strawberries.

The backyard patch sprawled farther each year, until it eventually stretched across the perimeter of the entire fence. Murl and June would start at the far end, working their way around until they reached the other side of the lawn, where Surl's shed rested. The sweet smell of the fruit danced in the sky with tobacco smoke and dust from the wood chips.

Wish he wouldn't smoke that ol' stuff, Murl tutted on a regular basis. Surl calls Muriel "Murl." Murl calls Cyril "Surl."

Surl! Stop smokin' that ol' stuff! she would bawl across the yard, scolding each time she sniffed it.

Yes, *Murl*, he would puff, snuffing the pipe out, only to light it again a half hour later, after she'd started on housework or cooking.

But to June, the garden wouldn't have been complete without that masculine-feminine mixology. Blue sky brushed white with clouds shaped like cotton balls and cyclones. Green grass, red berries, white house, white shed—the backyard smelled of freshness and life. Like the brown crayon, the box wouldn't have been complete without tobacco smoke and wood chips.

The sound of babbling bubbles from Rennie's River harmonized with the trickle of the little waterfall in the back corner, homemade by Surl. The wood stove in the shed crackled while traditional Newfoundland tunes floated from his Radio Shack AM dial. Accordion music when Surl felt like practicing. He and his brother, a seventh son of a seventh son, had played together frequently. Sometimes it was too painful to play, Surl missed him so much.

The day June got her period, Murl waddled over to Macpherson Junior High to pick her up early.

Mom, no. *Please* don't come and get me, June pleaded on the phone. I can walk home on my own.

Don't be fool-eesh, June, I'm comin' fer ya. You needs yer mudder da-day. She was so matter of fact about it that there was no point in arguing.

With Murl, what normally took June ten minutes was a one-hour walk home. Trickles of blood down her leg, dripping onto the sidewalk, leaving a trail behind her, mortified that someone would see them. June knew her mother only wanted to be there for her. But she couldn't help being embarrassed by her.

Now, Murl huffed and she puffed as they opened the front door. G'wan and get yourself cleaned up, and I'll bring ya some Aspirin and a hot water bottle for yer belly.

They lived in the side apartment of the mansion, but the owner was a prominent politician who was frequently out of town. They had bedrooms in the servants' quarters as well, so when the owners were away, they'd be asked to stay in the main house, which is where they were staying the day June got her period.

While Murl busied herself, June changed and then found her way to the backyard shed. Surl, puffing his pipe in peace, looked up from the shelf he was sanding. June sat on the raised stool at the workbench.

'Ow was school? he said, smoke pluming from his mouth above his head. Ryan's Fancy floated at low volume from the radio.

June shrugged, feeling, as usual, in tune with her father's quietly muffled frequency.

Want to 'elp me move the tomato plants into the beds? He gestured towards the greenhouse at the back of the shed.

June nodded. Wordlessly, together, they combed their fingers through the soil in the pots. Gently scooped the roots, cradled them in their palms, carried them over to nestle them into their beds. Patted the dirt with their palms, tucking them in for sleep and a fresh season.

They'll be red by next mont', mark my words. Surl winked a sparkly sky-blue eye at her. He puffed his pipe and June gave him a kiss on the cheek and went inside to let Murl dote on her.

In the early '90s, Murl convinced Surl to let her buy a waterbed, to help with her back issues.

Der s'posed to be right *soothing*, Surl. Like sleepin' on a *boat*. You'd like that, now, Surl. Wouldn't ya now? Sleepin' on a *boat*?

Surl, as usual, didn't say much in return. Just nodded. He'd slept on a boat before, that's for certain. Back in Bonavista, he'd sneak onto his uncle's dory from time to time, bobbing on the waves, sitting, mostly in silence, doing whatever his uncle asked him to.

Quite often, Surl lay back for a nap once his uncle said it was okay. It was a welcome escape from the intensity of his father, a stern schoolteacher whose presence raised Surl's blood pressure. Though he was left-handed, his father forced him to learn to write "right." He'd rap him on the knuckles until they bled, until his *R*s and *D*s and everything in between were curved and formed perfectly. His sharp nose, his thick black-framed glasses, his brow forever furrowed, his mouth eternally frowned . . . severe and condemning in every way. All the children of Bonavista feared Surl's father. Except for Murl. Surl first met Murl when her family moved from Arnold's Cove to Bonavista in 1938. She was eight years old, he twelve. She'd stick her tongue out behind his back any time she was scolded. Surl felt a harmonious wave wash through him every time he caught her doing it.

When Murl was fourteen, her father and brother drowned while out on the fishing boats. Weather took a turn, the boys took a tip. Surl's uncle was the one who delivered the news. Murl and her sister were shipped off to New York to work and send money back home. There was no other choice.

Murl lied to get a job at Macy's, telling them she had worked at Bowering's in St. John's. I worked in the gloves department, she lied. Charmed the manager, a fellow named Mr. Pearly Graye. He was smitten with her, and she with him. They were both enchanting and exuberant. He brought her flowers when her shifts ended. Took her to the swing clubs of Manhattan. Twirled her under his arm and swung her up into the air on dance floors all over the city. He wined her, he dined her, at all the best restaurants. Sardi's, even. Sang like Sinatra. All the old tricks, the most professional wooing, until she became Mrs. Muriel Graye.

Once she was his, he became a mean drunk. Pearly Graye loved to have a good time, but he didn't know when to stop. Even his sister warned Muriel that she needed to leave.

Pearly can't help himself, she said. He can't resist the alcohol.

So, finally, one night before Pearly got home from the bar, Muriel tossed her things into a suitcase and fled. She found employment at a private school for rich boys, and while there, decided to write to her old friend, her best friend and her one and only, Surl.

For two years they sent letters back and forth, rekindling their relationship and making plans.

Dearest Muriel, he wrote once. *Whenever I am underwater, you fish me out. You are the crest of my every wave.*

They married in the Central Court Building in Brooklyn in 1951 and made their way to St. John's, where they took a groundskeeping job and a housekeeping job for 74 Circular Road.

June was born in June of '52.

They lived there for thirty years, choosing to stay even after the politician sold the house, and they both had to find new work to pay the rent. It was their home. Murl and Surl spent summer evenings sitting on the back-patio porch swing, holding hands, listening to the river, watching the sunset.

Sometimes, June caught Murl with her head on Surl's shoulder.

Sometimes, muffled into his wife's windy hair, Surl hummed under his breath. He floated through much of life on passivity and a calm detachment, mostly just happy to be by Murl's side, or in his shed, or in his den, having a puff or scratching out music for one of his many compositions heard by no one beyond the walls of the great big house. On winter nights, if not in the shed, he sat in a brown recliner, looking at the handcrafted fireplace he'd constructed with charcoal plastic and foil strips that rotated and brushed the plastic, mimicking the crackle of flames.

Sometimes, Murl secretly watched him, from around the corner of the door or through the kitchen window, in awe of the satisfaction he got just from sitting in silence and solitude. Watching him this way filled Murl's soul with the reddest, sweetest strawberries.

Quiet and serene as he was, every now and then, Surl tossed a clever quip into the dinner-table conversation, just to surprise his girls.

Whadda ya think, Surl? Murl said, about two weeks after they got the waterbed. Of the waterbed? Do ya like the waterbed, Surl?

I don't know now, *Murl*, he teased. Every night I'm ridin' on the crest of a wave.

June snorted mashed potatoes out her nose and coughed them all over her place setting and she gave Surl a smack on the arm and he clapped his hand over his mouth and snickered.

Devils, the two o' ye, Murl said, pinching June's nose. Murl knew that when Surl was sassy, it meant he felt relaxed and safe. Das all right, I feels like I wants to t'row up every time I goes to sleep.

They all had a laugh, and the waterbed was removed within the next few days.

But sometimes, Murl worried about what was in Surl's head when he stared off into the fire.

Sometimes, Surl got agitated. In his later years, in particular, he had spells where he paced back and forth, wringing his hands, rubbing his head, his brow crunched in worry. Fear. Bracing himself for something. An old strap across the knuckles, perhaps.

Gentle Jesus, Surl, what in heaven's name have you got to worry about? Sure, he's got nothin' to worry about! She'd throw her arms in the air in exasperation. Eventually he'd calm down enough to sit in the living room recliner, where his angst would dissolve into manic tears, streaming down his face.

Wha's wrong wit' me? he'd moan, sobbing, gasping for breath like a child.

They took him for shock treatments, to kill the dread. Surl never spoke about his father. Never spoke about his feelings. Murl had always wondered, even as a child, what Surl's father was like behind closed doors in their home. But she never dared to ask.

Still, almost every evening, summer or autumn or winter, serene or tortured, Surl and Murl sat on the porch swing. Even if it was just for ten minutes. Whether Surl was humming or whether he was dead silent, staring into the distance.

When the diagnosis came, Murl was not prepared. She always did her best when he was calm and at ease. In these moments, she forgot to see herself as he saw her— brash, brazen, not a person to contend with.

I told him he shouldn't smoke those ol' t'ings, she sobbed to the doctor, June clutching her hand.

Surl's illness was quick. He refused treatment. When the time came, Murl and June sat on each side of him, on the bed, each holding a hand. He stared tranquilly into the distance, towards the horizon, beyond the horizon, a serenity across his face as if he was smoking his corncob pipe alone in the greenhouse.

They moved out shortly after Surl's passing. Thanks to a very modest life, Murl had enough to get herself a spot at Kenny's Pond Apartments.

Wha's we gonna do if we can't pick strawberries, June? We always picks berries, every summer.

We'll still pick berries, Mom. Promise.

Murl has lived in Kenny's Pond Apartments for about a year. In the first year after they move from Circular Road, the first year away from the backyard patch, June drives Murl to a U-Pick just outside of town, connected to the farmer's market. The July day is twenty-five degrees, and Murl is already wheezing when the cart attached to the truck sinks under her weight as she steps up, so much so that the few passengers already on board have to grasp the rail behind the benches they're seated on. The truck only gets so far out into the field before letting the pickers off. In midfield, finally, June can't hold Murl up any longer. Murl grips her chest, her fingers sinking into the plump breast flesh.

I can't . . . draw a breat' . . .

It's okay, Mom. June eases her mother towards the earth and crouches next to her. Murl hasn't been the same since Surl passed. She clutches her mother's hand. Presses their cheeks together. Relax. I'm here. June closes her eyes. She feels Murl's clenched body relax. Dad's here, too.

The truck tears back towards the farmer's market to find help, bouncing over the strawberry plants, little red strawberries exploding under the truck's weight, leaving behind a trail of red blotches like the day June got her period.

Murl's wheezing breath slows. The hot sun cooking her broad body, she lets her gaze blur, soften, the bright yellow sunlight bleaching into white. Her hand falls from her chest, down to the earth. She is serene in her solitude. Her fingers sink into the soil, the dirt that was always in the grooves of Surl's fingers now in hers. Her head on Surl's shoulder, they are on the porch swing, riding on the crest of a wave.

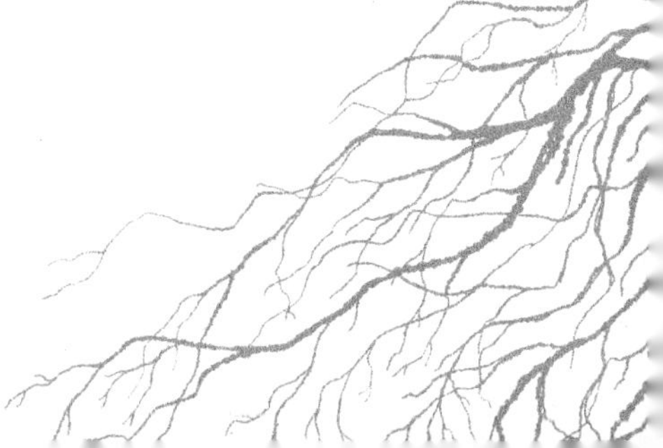

LULU

When I was little, Maman doted on me. Dressed me like I was a doll, my outfits matching hers, my hair in buns on top of my head. Tutus and bodysuits and Parisian frocks. She ran her knuckles down my back so my posture was always perfect. Spied on my pliés and arabesques and made sure I practiced them Every . . . Single . . . Day. I wanted to please her. I idolized her. She was beautiful in every way. Her wide, innocent eyes and her balletic posture. Her soul seemed to bloom flowers. I loved to dance, just like her. If I worked hard enough, just maybe I could be as good as she was someday.

My childhood in Europe was a fairy tale, and not the Grimms' kind, the Disney kind (like, puke). The story of how my parents met was rooted in every breath I took. They performed it so many times, it was tattooed to my guts.

We met on the riverbank of the Seine, Maman would sigh, gazing heart eyed into Papa's eyes.

I was in Paris for a conference with the Congress of Psychology, Papa would add, lacing his fingers into hers. *Walking back to my* hotel one evening, I was captivated by the sight of Élodie, dancing along the water's edge.

I did not even notice him! Maman's laugh sang as she stroked her fingers softly down his muscular arm (which was almost the same size as her tiny torso).

She was mellifluous (Papa loved that word) and melodic, he would respond. A willow in the wind. Her long, silky, auburn mane whipping and dancing through the air. I imagined the wisps of her hair extending, reaching farther and farther until they wrapped themselves around me and pulled me towards her. There was nothing I could do about it. It was destiny.

He always did the same shoulder shrug at that part.

And then, Maman continued, he invited me for a cocktail in Montmartre!

And she said oui! Papa marvelled.

Pleased as a freshly licked cat! she twittered, linking her arm into Papa's. We strolled through the cobblestone streets, sat on the lawn in front of Sacré-Coeur . . .

The white limestone shining on us like planetary guidance, bathing us in angelic light, as if the universe was begging us to kiss, said Papa, looking down into Maman's eyes as she swooned back up at him, agog.

When I reached puberty, I would interrupt their story around this part and pretend to barf, and overlap what they were saying and roll my eyes.

And you stayed there, on the lawn of Sacré-Coeur, until the sun caressed the next day awake—I know, I know, okay? You two gross me out.

The scripture of their love story started to taste like artificial sweetener. A vain imitation of the real thing. I was almost hoping for Grimm.

Maman was devastated to leave Europe. We'd lived in Paris for a while—where I was born in 1979—then Amsterdam and Venice. And eventually we landed in Prague, when I was eight. The last place we lived before coming here.

I liked my life in Prague. I didn't have many friends. Two, to be exact. But we were a tight trio. At least I had friends in Prague. Me, Froggo (real name Frederik) and Marcella spent all of our free time together, wandering the winding streets, quoting Camus:

Live to the point of tears.
Should I kill myself, or have a cup of coffee?
But in the end one needs more courage to live than to kill himself.

We prided ourselves on being melodramatic emo teenagers.

I was thirteen when I learned we were moving to St. John's. Papa was offered a top position in the psychology department at the university here. He'd been itching to try something new for a while. As was his nature. I was only given a couple of months to say goodbye to Prague. It was 1992, the year of the cod moratorium. Everyone who lived in St. John's was depressed because of the closure of the fishery, which, until then, had pretty much justified Newfoundland's existence. Society was built upon the success of the fishing industry. They didn't know anything else. Their songs revolved around the fish and the water. It's how most were employed for many centuries, it was their biggest export.

My schoolmates seemed narrow-minded and overly innocent, but also equally crass. I didn't "get" most of the people I went to school with. I admit it, I did feel superior to them. They didn't have anything to talk about except drinking in the woods, who hooked up with who, how crappy the weather was, how deadly summer is, how deadly George Street is, how much Newfoundland sucked. At least I agreed with them on that. But I couldn't *say* anything, God forbid. I couldn't agree with them. I wasn't a Newfoundlander. Only Newfoundlanders are allowed to talk shit about Newfoundland.

I remember the first time we ever drove past this house, not too long after we arrived. We were staying in the house of another prof in the psychology department, temporarily, while he was on sabbatical for the semester. Me sitting in the back seat, Maman in the front, craning her neck, peering out and up.

Someday, I will own zis 'ouse, she said, calm and carefree, like it was nothing. She used to notice the Dancing House in Prague the same way. The Dancing House was built on the site of an apartment building that was destroyed during the 1945 U.S. bombing. The land was decrepit and void of all life until 1960 but was eventually reconstructed into two pristine buildings next to each other. One represented Fred Astaire, one was meant to be Ginger Rogers, curled into Fred's side.

New life growing from devastation, Maman said as she stared up at the concrete. It was like her mantra. Like she needed to feel connected to tragedy in order to feel fully alive. Putting so much meaning into every little thing in life. A bruise on an orange meant it needed love. A dying leaf on a plant needed a funeral.

I remember her saying, The most twisted parts of us are the most fascinating ones, my Lulu. Without the ones with the darkness, the world would be a boring place. We must put as much attention into the pain as we do for the joy.

Her depressive tendencies were infrequent when I was a child, when she was just my pretty, young mother who bloomed along with fresh air, sunshine, a rainbow, a beach, an ice cream, her childlike wonder for all of life's lovely things. She floated on air. Grace Kelly, but with thick, black eyeliner and giant black brows above wide, brown eyes. Grace Kelly with darkness.

Occasionally though, I would catch her sitting and staring blankly into the expanse. Like she was yearning for something but didn't know whether that thing even existed.

Leading up to when we moved to St. John's, the gloom hung around her for longer periods of time. Her shoulders slumped more than usual. Her bones began to stick sharper from beneath her skin.

We'll find our way in Canada, Papa promised. They've so much more space than we have! You'll have your own personal oasis! Your essence will bring spring. He wrapped his big arms around her, enveloped her into him, reassuring her it would all be fine. She loved him, and she believed him, and she relied on him to give her strength.

By the time we'd arrived in Newfoundland and first drove past that house, the vision of growing her own oasis had become like her mantra. Her new, sole (and soul) focus. My father continued to shape how she moved through her world. He'd been doing it for decades. He knew just what to say to bring back her light. He was always reassuring her. It must have been exhausting for him.

It's not even for sale, I grumbled. It's way too big for the three of us. Completely unnecessary.

Now, living in this grey and foggy city, I'd seemed to curse myself by somehow manifesting the darkness my friends and I had celebrated in our Camus readings. Back when I had friends. Here, I didn't really know anyone except my over-the-top, tortured-artist slash intellectual set of co-creators. Sadly, I needed them to help me find my way.

A month later, we drove past the house again. Wouldn't you know it? For Sale.

Otto! We *must*! Say we will. *Please*.

Élodie, mon oiseau, really . . . he said to Maman, glancing in the rearview mirror at me, to let me know he'd been listening to my objections. Is this necessary?

I rolled my eyes. He was just putting on a show, too. He was as much of an actor as she was. Buying this house would be fucking *stupid*! I yelled. I couldn't help it. The money you'd waste on this, we could move back to Prague.

Lulu! Language, please! Otto, you said we would build an oasis. This is it. I will fill this place with love. Our new life, our new world. We need to embrace this place, Lulu. This is our future.

A week later, we were moving in. I couldn't fucking believe it.

The ballerinas will come through here. Maman danced from the door to the studio entrance at the top of the stairs to the basement, as if she was unrolling the red carpet of the movie of our lives in this mansion full of ghosts.

It didn't take long before the antiques started coming into the house. It became more museum-like each week.

Elle, the spending is getting out of control. You have to stop this, said Papa.

Christmas is soon! I want it to be magical! She danced around the foyer, dusting the grandfather clock, the radio from the '20s, the Edwardian end tables.

She didn't stop. Each antique through the front door was another hour Papa spent away from the house. Over time, his "faculty dinners" became much more frequent.

Much like their romance, my parents' parting of ways was operatic.

Please! Maman begged, grabbing his shoulders, sinking to the floor as he headed out again. Please stay home with me ce soir.

Stop, Élodie. He would shake her off of him. Please. Have some dignity, for God sakes.

Her novelty had finally worn off. Her desperation eclipsed her charm. He didn't love her anymore. There was nothing anyone could do. Yet she clung.

I heard him on the phone one night. The door of his office left open, just a smidge. He was leaned against the wall underneath the steep gable window, the A-frame ceiling just brushing the top of his head. I crept down the hallway on my hands and knees, careful not to make a peep on the heavily cushioned bright-red carpet. I plucked up the hallway phone, stealth of a spy, and put my other hand over the bottom of the receiver, to mute my breathing.

Yes. I will do it soon, he said into the receiver.

When? said the woman on the other end of the line. Her voice sounded young.

By the end of the week.

The sucker punch to my guts nearly gave me away as I gulped back a gasp. I held my breath and laid the receiver back on its cradle. I could see Papa, the office door just slightly ajar. He glanced towards the doorway and I ducked out of view. Crawled and scurried back to my bedroom. Shut the door and turned on Nirvana and leaned my back against the door and shoved a pillow in my face to let the tears soak it. I lay awake all night with knots in my stomach.

Papa left Maman in a puddle on the floor the next day.

I've tried to speak to you, Élodie. Many times. You don't listen, he said, shaking her off his leg. Be strong, he said. Nurture yourself. And he closed the door behind him. We'd moved here in August, into this house in October, and he was gone before 1993 was a month over, leaving me to take care of her. Me. Age thirteen.

When she first brought Brandon Lee home, I wanted to murder him. Shitting on the floor. Flapping his feathers loudly. Caw-cawwwwing to other members of the cosmopolitan Corvidae family of oscine passerine birds that we'd been studying in environmental science. If I'd had any friends, I would have been humiliated to have them over. I could just imagine if I invited this girl over that I hung around with at school sometimes. Tanya, who was viciously territorial and jealous and insecure and looked down her nose at everyone. It'd be all over school if Tanya knew I lived in Dr. Dolittle's house.

I stayed up late picking up after *her*: Maman. Collecting tipped-over glasses. Wiping up vodka and dabbing up crow shit before the ballet students arrived. Protecting her reputation. Hiding this mess of a functioning alcoholic from the tiny gossipy city of St. John's. Scrambling, scurrying, all so sweet Élodie could keep some dignity in the community. It was my only chance at survival and I resented her for it.

Maman had some fucked-up codependence on Brandon Lee. He dropped random shiny objects around as "gifts." Bits of tinfoil. Coins. She was so happy when he brought the ring back to her.

I lost my shit. Yelled at her, Do you think just because he brought that thing back, it's some kind of sign that Otto's coming back? Don't you know, that's just what crows and magpies do? Bring shiny objects? It doesn't *mean* anything. Papa is not coming back. He's fucking *gone*. Brandon Lee is not a replacement for him, he's a fucking *crow*. Get a life. You're a ghost.

Her face fell and I stared at her, drunk on the couch, black mascara streaming down her cheeks. She'd reached a film noir, Camus level of gloom that, in that moment, I kind of sadistically enjoyed, and then I cursed myself for being so cruel. I regretted yelling so harshly. She looked so pathetic, sitting there crying. Was I a monster? Screaming at her like that? I sat next to her. I cried. She put her arms around me and we cried together. It was a turning point. It released something that had been floating between us.

Let me tuck you in, I said.

I'm sorry, Lulu, she said. Weak.

It's okay. I led her up the stairs and told her to get ready for bed and I'd get her some water and Tylenol. Which I did.

I listened carefully as I got in bed that night. Her room was silent.

In the days that followed, there seemed to be a calm after the storm. A break in the grey clouds and thick air pressure. I was around the corner, once again finding myself listening in on a phone call. For the first time in years, I heard brightness in her voice.

That was two years ago, and things have been relatively stable. The crying spurts have had longer periods of time between them. She hasn't been drinking, at least not enough so that I can smell it. I am eighteen now, in my final year of high school. Next year, I hope I can go to the National Ballet School in Toronto. God doesn't exist, yet that doesn't stop me from praying to Jesus every night that being accepted will happen.

The choirs are about to arrive in Newfoundland. Maman is excited to host them. She will be busy. She will be around people. Why am I so worried?

ÉLODIE

Where is he?

What is he doing?

Is he thinking of me at all?

Why doesn't he love me anymore?

Does he even care at all anymore?

Why wasn't I enough?

I think of him compulsively. Gnawing at my brain, drilling into my heart, infecting me, torturing me, endlessly. I float through life in a dense malaise, undulating between broiling anxiety and flat soullessness, bobbing along on an endless black sea that will eventually swallow me into a black void.

For so long, he sparked something within me that defined my essence, my driving force. As long as I knew he was in my corner, the despair that has taunted me for my entire life could be blown away.

I could feel him slipping away before he actually left. I sensed his annoyance, it prickled my skin. But I never every believed he would leave me. Not ever. Our love was profound and deep. But I suppose all fairy tales end in some way or another.

The rejection felt like an axe chop to my very essence. The sharpest sword, slicing up through my body, the day he left me in a pool on the floor. The hot flash of shock, of betrayal, of abandonment. I know I will never grow back together inside. Every memory only deepens the gash or adds another one, one on top of the other, slicing up my insides so they're composed of scars. The more time that passes, the deeper my grief's roots expand. No more strong hands to rub my shoulders in the mornings and the evenings. No one for me to curl into in the middle of the night. For hours on end, I imagine what his life is like without me—with his new woman, I was certain. A better, smarter, sexier woman than I, an ugly, sagging, miserable, aging, unfuckable bag of bones.

The vodka lays a warm shawl around my shoulders, making me feel fuzzy inside, sending me towards slumber, the only time I am free from the anguish in my waking life. If I'm lucky. I dream of him often, only to wake up smiling and remember that he's gone, and then my days become haunted. I don't know where I am anymore. What are these strange surroundings? I don't recognize my life without him here. Sometimes I pretend he's just away at a conference and will be returning the next day. That helps, temporarily. The comfort of denial.

I struggle to find slices of pleasure. I know objectively what should bring this, but I can't seem to latch on to these things in any sort of meaningful way. I write lists of things I should be grateful for.

My ballet students, teetering into the studio on Saturdays and Sundays in their darling pink tutus and slippers, wiggling in their tights as I adjust their chubby little hands into graceful formations, the way I used to do with Lulu when she was a small child.

My antique shopping. I drift through the shop on a very regular basis, perusing the shelves, grazing my fingers over the items, weaving through belongings of strangers from the past, attaching my energy to theirs, then bringing them back to the house. The antiques are like company in some twisted way. I am held captive to the thing that destroyed my marriage. It's unhealthy, yet still comforting.

Brandon Lee. It seems insane, I'm sure. Living with a crow in the house. That kooky European should be in an asylum! But I feel connected to him. Like we watch out for each other. It's a mystical, inexplicable connection that somehow gives me strength. Perhaps it's his darkness. It is familiar. Perhaps it's his intellect. What he represents, in mythology: prophecy. Fortune-telling. The future. Keeping him alive gives me some dark hope for the future?

My Lulu. My reason for existing. She grows increasingly resentful every day. Her strength, her intellect, her practicality, reminds me of My Otto. Of our life together. The only thing I feel more sharply than melancholy, more profoundly than my desire to drink, is the guilt and shame I carry for being a simply abysmal excuse for a mother. I want to be better, but I don't have the strength. I'm selfish, I know it. I hate myself for being so useless. What if our relationship can never be repaired? What if I lose her too? I can't bear it.

It takes every ounce of my strength to call Melanie. I don't want to. I want to keep drinking, keep crying. Hold on to the things that comfort me. But the things that comfort me are killing me. I must try. If not for myself, for my daughter. What would I want her to do when she's heartbroken? Not live the rest of her life this way, that is for certain. I stand. I stretch. I inhale, I exhale. I pick up the phone. None of these visiting choristers know anything about me. With them, I can have a fresh start. I can resurrect, I can reform, I can rise from the ashes, just like the Brandon Lee in the movie. I will draw strength all my life from this house and beyond—my ballerinas, my crow, my plants, my animals. My daughter. I must try, with everything I have, to escape this prison.

JOE'S PINK POPSICLE

I remember the drippy, sticky coolness of the pink Popsicle between my lips, on my tongue, slipping down my throat. Sometimes it was so hot outside that I'd suck and swallow too fast and get a headache. The pain would jab me in the back of the throat and trickle through my jaw, up to my temples. An electric seizure of sorts. I'd sit on the curb, grasping my head, leaning over my knees. Drop the Popsicle sticks between the slats of the storm drain down into the sewer and harshly exhale hot breath from my mouth, rubbing my temples, exorcizing the pain from my body.

I slide the ice cube over Joe's lips, dry from the hospital and from breathing through his mouth. Tubes, hard and plastic, shoved up his nostrils, probably burrowing into his frontal lobe. I think about the giant colourful poster showing the anatomy of the brain in our science lab, and I wonder how a poke in his frontal lobe will affect him. Could it reverse the damage done to his cerebellum when his skull cracked off of the sidewalk?

When I was a child, Joe would take me to the park and sit on the swing next to me. We'd compete to see who could get higher, which he always did, which made me huff and puff, my bottom lip quivering, hot tears of defeat spilling from my eyes.

"Well, girl," Joe would say, "sure, whaddya expect? A big fat fella like me next to a tiny tweeny dust mite like you? I got a lotta weight to me, ya know. O' course I'm gonna fly higher!"

Then he'd release the chains and hoist himself off his swing, lurching his body through the air and (staggeringly) sticking the landing, his Zellers-brand sneakers slapping onto the gravel. Before I knew it, he was behind me, then beneath me, giving me an underduck. My body felt as if it'd soar right off the seat and I'd squeal, the sensation that my heart was about to sprout wings and fly free, right out of my mouth, up to meet the clouds, until it was suddenly clutched by the force of gravity, yanking me back towards earth. I always felt a tingle between my legs as I dropped towards the ground.

Joe is only ten years older than me. Now, I am twenty-five and he is thirty-five. I'm moving to Montreal at the end of the summer. I've gone through school, a music degree, an education degree, I'm about to start grad school and Joe . . . has been exactly the same the whole time I've known him.

When I was six and he was sixteen, it seemed like a big age gap. Traipsing around our neighbourhood, he never felt like a parent, and not even quite like an uncle. Yet not like an older brother, either. In Venice Pizza one time, after we got off the swings, we ran into one of his friends. Bobby Butler.

"Y'at bah, Joeyyyy?" Bobby flicked Joe right in the forehead with his yellow-stained finger. I remember noticing a hangnail scratch on Joe's eyelid. Bobby shoved Joe backwards after the flick, and Joe stumbled into the pizza counter.

"Nudding b'y, Bobby." Joe rubbed his head where he'd been flicked. "Just out with me little sister." He glanced at me and in his eyes flashed *I'm sorry for saying you're my sister* regret.

Bobby backed out of Venice with his pizza box in his hand. He glared at Joe the whole time, squinting. Just before he left, he pointed his two fingers at his own eyes and then pointed them at Joe.

"Arsehole," Joe muttered under his breath as he dug in his pockets for a few bucks. "Slice o' pepperoni, please," he told the cashier.

"Why was he like that to you?" I asked Joe, as we walked towards Needs Convenience a few doors down.

Joe rolled and folded and finished his pizza in three swallows and closed the lid on the box. "He's just a bully, das all." He wiped the grease from his face with his hands, which didn't really get rid of the grease at all, it only spread it further around on his cheeks. He hoisted open the door of Needs. He bought me a pink Popsicle and we crossed the road and sat on the steps of the Colonial Building. I remember noticing the bird shit splattered all over the majestic marble columns. Making a mockery of the bullies who built the Colonial Building.

"Don't let the bullies get ya, Megsy. Life lesson."

I cracked my Popsicle in half and gave one stick to him.

The doctor tells us that Joe has suffered traumatic brain injury.

"There is bruising as a result of the assault. If he lives, he may experience cognitive deficits—confusion, shortened attention span, amnesia, problem-solving or judgement issues, a loss of sense of time and space . . ."

Some of the doctor's words make sense to me, but most just sound like warbles. Jibber jabber.

Mom stands next to me, and I swear I can feel her heartbeat in my eardrums. I remember the day she told me Joe would be living with us for a while.

"Why?" I asked, befuddled.

"Well he's here almost all the time anyway, snacking on our stuff, watching our TV," Mom said. "And his mother's got a hard time of it. He's a nice young fella, just needs some support, that's all."

“But, we barely have room here for the three of us, let alone another person,” I argued. Mom, my sister and I had moved into the basement apartment on Circular Road after my dad died. Mom didn’t want to care for the lawn anymore, and she only had one income now. “It’ll be cozy,” she said. I always liked the creepy feeling in that apartment, and in that house. And I liked the landlady, an eccentric French woman who baked us the most incredible croissants and profiteroles. Whenever we had a lemonade stand, the neighbours flocked and we made a mint.

I tried to think of the number of times I’d seen Joe’s mother and could remember exactly twice. I spied her across the street, stumbling into their house after a “late shift.” That’s what Joe said, when I asked him the next day where his mom was coming home from last night. He didn’t look up from the dirt when he said it. They lived in a small apartment over on Hayward Avenue, and I’d met Joe while my sister and I were at the park one day. The other time I saw Joe’s mom was on Regatta Day. We had tables set up in front of the house, selling lemonade, French pastries and old household items we no longer needed.

“I always loved books,” she slurred, struggling to focus on the back cover of an original edition of Judy Blume’s *Superfudge*. I remember thinking Fudge looked like a kid version of Joe.

Mom had invited her in for a cup of coffee that day, and she sat at our kitchen table and manoeuvred her face towards the cup. “’Dere’s ghosts in here.” She looked at the ceiling, and towards the cellar, suspiciously.

“Yes,” Mom said. “Sure we knows there’s ghosts in here! We’re all friendly with each other.”

It was very shortly after that visit that Mom told me Joe would be moving in. Mom set up a little bedroom for him in the cellar. Joe was happy to be asked for help shovelling, or going to the grocery store, or driving our junky Corolla to the garage. He even learned to make goulash, and he got pretty good at it, too.

". . . motor deficits may include paralysis or weakness, delays in getting started, tremors, swallowing problems . . ."

I picture him flying off the swing when I was six.

". . . perceptually, he may have changes in hearing, vision, taste, smell, touch—difficulty understanding where limbs are in relation to the body, vision problems. Insofar as communication and language deficits, he may have various forms of aphasia, meaning he could have difficulty speaking and understanding speech, choosing the right words to say, or he may have difficulty reading or writing—"

"Well that's nothing new." I blurt it out before I realize what I'm saying.

The doctor pauses only for a split second.

". . . impaired abilities with activities of daily living, such as dressing and eating, problems with organization, shopping or paying bills."

I snort back laughter.

"Megan!" Mom whispers, vicious, jabbing me in the ribs.

Joe lived on Cheez Whiz and crackers and Pepsi. He wore the same Coors Light T-shirt until it literally fell apart at the seams and ceased to clothe his body anymore.

"Joe may also have social difficulties, such as impaired social capacity resulting in difficult interpersonal relationships, difficulties in making and keeping friends or understanding and responding to the nuances of social situations . . ."

When I was ten and Joe was twenty, he took me to see *Follow That Bird* in the movie theatre. Standing at the popcorn counter, he leaned down to me as we approached the front of the line. "She's cute, i'n't she?" I shrugged my shoulders.

"We're seein' *Follow Dat Bird* here, with me little sister." He nodded his head towards me.

The girl smiled. "That's nice. What can I get you?"

Joe tried to wink at the girl, but he didn't know how to wink, and instead ended up doing a weird double-blink kind of half-seizure-looking manoeuvre. The girl crumpled her brow.

"Oh, ahhh, just ahhh, two medium popcorns and two P-p-p-epsi. P-p-p-please."

The girl rolled her eyes and went off to fill our buckets and cups.

I felt nothing short of devastated for Joe. He didn't say a word until we arrived back at our house on Circular Road, where he went right to his "bedroom," and stayed there for the rest of the night.

I remember the night Joe died. My flight to Montreal was supposed to be the next day. We'd made all the arrangements for him to come home, even though he never did regain consciousness. I remember thinking back to Joe, on the swing, releasing the chains. Standing outside the hospital, I exhaled, harshly, hot breath from my mouth, digging my fingers hard into my temples, desperate to purge the pain from my body.

Joe didn't have a cent to his name. Not a thing to leave behind besides a raggedy Coors Light T-shirt that he got for free out of a box of beer. He was bullied, he never had any luck with the ladies, he never had any real friends. But he never let any of that make him a shitty person. I believe he was happy. With the little nook he found with us, a little space of his own, the chance to be a bit of a help, Joe was content. He got into a life-changing accident that resulted in major brain trauma, and that was the time he chose to underduck out of this world.

Joe had it right, in lots of ways.

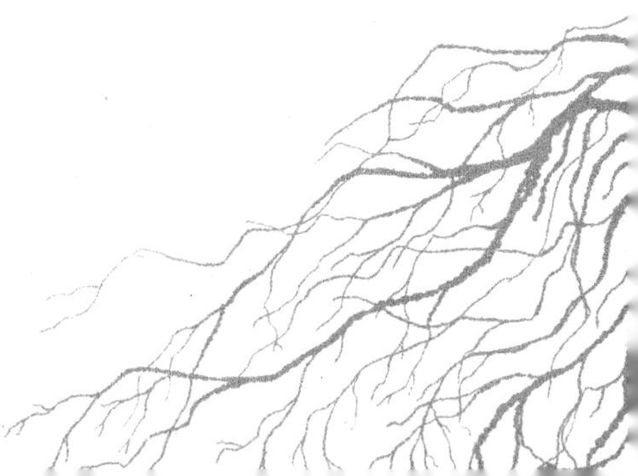

CROSSED LINES

Yes, maid. Y'huh, I got a new coat ordered from the Sears cat'log now.

Y-huh, yes now. Whas it like?

Hello? I say into the receiver. I don't recognize these voices.

Oh, 'tis a nice bright-red colour, white fur around the hood.

Y-huh.

Hello?? Helloooo???

Nothing.

They can't hear me. I'm trying to call Tryphena. I need to know what she's wearing to school tomorrow. I've got the phone cord hauled around the kitchen door, over to the dining room, Dad's bawlin' at me to go to bed out of it, and I can't even call her 'cause there's two old biddies talking about their new Sears coats on the phone.

Dat sounds nice, Mary, red.

Yes, maid. I never had a red coat before!

Dat'll look right nice on you, Mary.

I am stuck in a moment of indecision. Something about listening in on their conversation feels sinful, and I do the "Hail Mary, full of grace" cross on my chest that the sisters made us do at Sunday school. That should cover me, right? I think the lady who bought the red coat sounds like the woman who lives diagonal to us, in the big mansion on the corner of the rich part of Circular Road and Rennie's Mill Road. She lives there with her husband and two kids, and random people who live in the apartments. Her kid Bobby is a grade ahead of me. He's a bit of a skeet but in a hot way. But no . . . this red-coat woman sounds older than Bobby's mom . . . maybe . . . Oh, who am I kidding? I could be eavesdropping on any townie lady filling her cart with turnips and potatoes. A lot of them sound remarkably similar.

Tryphena said earlier today that she would wear her Ikeda international-flag jeans to school tomorrow, so I'd better not wear *my* Ikeda international-flag jeans to school tomorrow. Personally, I don't see why it's such a big deal because they're different colours, anyways. Hers are forest green, mine are red.

When I was a kid, like maybe five, we got a prank phone call at the house. I was wearing my red cords. The woman on the phone asked me what my mommy and daddy were doing. I told her my mommy was playing piano and daddy was putting my brothers to bed. The woman asked what I was wearing. This made me feel strange. Uhhh. I remember looking down. My red cords. Oh yeah? she said. Put your hand between your legs there. My face burned hot and I actually started to put my hand between my legs before I realized that I have the power here. I have to go now, I said, and slammed the phone back down on its base. I was disturbed. I felt shaky. I went to find Mom. I interrupted her piano practice.

Mom, I said, some weird lady just called here.

Who?

I don't know.

Well, what did she sound like?

Like an old hag, I said. Her voice was gruff. She sounded like any old woman with a Newfoundland accent.

Mom looked concerned. Well, you know how sometimes you pick up the phone to make a call, and you're listening to someone else's conversations? The lines get crossed?

Yeah.

Was it that?

No . . . it wasn't that. It was only me and her on the phone. She was asking me questions and I answered.

What did she ask you?

I burned hot again.

It's okay, honey, what did she say?

I told her. I told her about the hand between the legs.

Mom asked Dad if he knew who it could be. Nothing was ever said of the call again. There's something about a phone call . . . even though the person isn't physically next to you, they're in your *ear*. In your *mind*.

You gon' just use the same coat ya did last year?

Oh my God, they're still talking about coats.

Yes, maid. Gerl have a cow now, I goes 'n buys a new coat for no reason.

Tut tut oh g'wan b'y Gerl, don't be so fool-eesh.

Y'huh.

Don't be so stingy b'y, Gerl.

The two women cackle, the pitch getting higher and higher until they cry. Poor old Gerald.

Sometimes I'm not sure if I should trust Tryphena. I think she's my friend. I mean, I'm glad she hangs out with me. She's good for my reputation. And she's nice to me and everything, it's just . . . sometimes she's a bit of a boss-hog. Like this one time, we went into the cafeteria to find a spot to sit, and I suggested, What about that table in the corner? and she, like, *glared* at me. No, she said. Why? I said. Isn't it obvious? she said. No, I said. Tryphena just huffed and crossed her arms and rolled her eyes and stormed towards a table right in the middle of the room. She just wanted to be literally the centre of attention. Probably she knows that my red Ikeda international-flag jeans look nicer than her forest-green ones. And then she called me that night, and she told me that from now on, when she wants to sit in the middle, we sit in the middle. She said it in my *ear*. In my *mind*. I went to sleep thinking about the way her "instructions" made me feel. And let me tell you, it was not a nice feeling.

We just finished studying a book called *The Scarlet Letter* in English class the other day. It's about a woman named Hester Prynne who gets pregnant by a man she's not married to. As punishment, she has to walk around with a big letter *A* (for *adultery*) on the front of her dress. She has to stand on a scaffold for three hours while the town makes fun of her. Many of the other women are angered by her beauty and quiet dignity. I like to think that I'm Hester in this scenario, and Tryphena represents the jealous, petty women in the crowd.

One of the major themes in the book is shame. Hester's shame, but also the shame of the man who impregnated her. Guilt is another theme. Hester's husband, who she thought was lost at sea, was actually off gallivanting around when Hester got pregnant by the other guy (who—spoiler alert—was a *priest*!). Anyways, they all felt guilty. But why?

I felt guilty for disappointing Tryphena. Like if I can't reach her tonight (because I can't stop listening to these two old biddies talking about a new Sears coat), and I misunderstood what she meant about the Ikeda international-flag jeans and, like, our lines got crossed somehow. But why? Isn't this a free world? Can't I wear whatever I want?

Buy yourself a new coat! I scream it into the phone, even though they can't hear me. I want Tryphena to encourage me to wear what I want, the way those two women on the phone are supporting each other. I felt shame over the woman asking me to put my hands between my legs. But why? She's the one who was being a *perv*. She's the one who should feel *shame*, and lots of it. I am my own person. I am not letting some pervy old bag, or bossy jealous friend, make me feel bad about myself for no good reason.

Well, maid, s'pose I better go ta bed out of it, says the biddy with the new red coat on the way.

Yes, maid, y'huh, me too.

Go look t'rough da Sears catalogue now! Tomorrow we goes down. Gerl won't know.

They both squawk, in peals of laughter.

Oh my Jesus, some funny.

Y'huh.

All right, talk to ya later, maid.

Yes, night now, maid. God bless.

And don't get me started on God! I scream it into the phone, but they can't hear me. They've hung up, leaving me free to call Tryphena.

ÉLODIE

Melanie's warmth brings sunshine to my soggy existence. The newborn focus brings fresh energy and a possibility of reformation.

My dear, she says on the phone, we're so lucky to have you joining us.

Of course, I will make profiteroles for the meeting. They are my specialty! It will be a chance to bring some of my country to you, I tell Melanie. Thank you for inviting me.

My dear, you're most welcome. See you next week now.

It seemed an oddity to me, when we moved here, that the people of St. John's used such terms of endearment towards complete and utter strangers. Peculiar expressions, such as: My love, my ducky, my treasure.

And yet, I noticed the looks they gave me: You are different. You are not from here. Where you from then? they'd say, their brows furrowed, looking me up and down. I had overheard them ask other people the same thing, searching for a connection to a relative or a friend of theirs who grew up in the same town or somewhere across the bay. Always piecing together their ancestry. With me, there were no blood connections. I was the eccentric European ballerina who lived in the mansion on the corner. Inaccessible. Off in her own bubble. If not for my ballet studio, I would have been a complete outcast. I didn't do myself any favours, of course, the years after Otto left.

My story had leaked into the community and trickled through town. St. John's loves gossip. Part of my fear in joining the committee is that I will be shunned when I step into the room. I imagine them staring at me, whispering to each other, making me feel unwelcome and unloved. I cannot bare any more rejection. It would be the last tree chop. I would crawl into the basement and let the tree roots eat me alive.

I hang up the phone and write down the details of the meeting. Then I immediately begin to sift flour, form and knead the dough, the coolness sinking into the wrinkles in my hands, noticing the pleasure and peace that radiates inside me, simply from preparing a patisserie from my homeland, in my own house. Sometimes all one needs is one moment. For one tiny thing to happen. I sense Lulu walk past the kitchen door. She does not come in. Pauvre fille, she must have been afraid she was seeing some kind of illusion! Her mother? Not drunk? Or smoking? Or crying? Imagine that. She does not speak to me, and I let her pass, hoping she feels a tiny bit of promise as well.

I arrive at the committee meeting wearing a red dress with matching red Dior lipstick, sent from my sister in Paris. The dress is a little looser on me than is ideal. I will try to gain some weight. The profiteroles are carefully displayed on my finest platter, an 1875 Royal Doulton. Approximately twenty other women stand around the room, conversing and laughing. The room is aflutter. I add my plate to a long table adorned with every type of Newfoundland dessert square you can imagine. Date squares, lemon squares,

Queen Anne squares. And not just squares! Snowballs. Lassy mogs. Shortbread. Is it Christmas? This is most certainly a good place to gain some weight. I recognize many of the women I have seen about town and worried they've whispered about me.

A woman I don't recognize swoops into the room, clapping her hands to get everyone's attention. Good evening, ladies! Thank you so much for coming. My name is Doreen Day, and I am the director of Festival 500 choral festival. We are going to have such a special time together planning this historic event. Please, get your plates and find a seat and we'll get started.

Doreen's aura is pastel pink and purple, like Paris in springtime. Her pink lipstick, blushed cheeks, and fluffed hair a fresh bouquet blasting away any grey.

The women's paper plates brim with sweets, their Styrofoam cups piping hot with Red Rose tea.

Now, ladies, I'd first like to start by telling you a little about why and how Festival 500 was conceived. Even Doreen's speaking voice is musical. Listening to her, watching her, a Monet splashes to life inside me.

I, like all of you, like everyone from this place, was devastated at the announcement of the moratorium, just a few years ago. She looks at the floor, clasping her hands together. It felt as if a gaping dark hole was left, hovering over us and around us, robbing us of our livelihood. What was our purpose now? The loss of the beloved fishery was the loss of our identity. The wound is still raw.

The ladies murmur in agreement. Loss of identity: I understood this feeling, of course.

But, my friends, Doreen continues, life goes on. Loss is all around us, we can't deny it. Death—of a person, of an industry, of any love—is life's only certainty, is it not? We all must find the strength to carry on. There is so much life left, despite tragedy. For me, my love of traditional Newfoundland music pulled me through this particular loss. Music moves me through sadness, gladness. Brings life to full colour. Like all art.

Doreen scans the room and looks directly at me. We have a world-class prima ballerina in our presence today, ladies. Élodie, I know you relate to what I say.

I can only muster a nod. I am filled with pride. I feel valued.

In my grief, Doreen continues, I eventually realized that we here are known as much for our culture, our music, our storytelling, as we are for our fishing. I mean, virtually everyone here plays music for goodness' sakes. We do not segregate based on the level of achievement. We welcome anyone who wants to take part! This should be shouted from the rooftops! And so, from all of this, I began to plan, to sketch out what a choral festival could look like. I went to the men with the money, she laughs. I pitched it. And, she winks at us, they gave me the money.

The women in the room cheer and holler!

We will celebrate five hundred years of the discovery of Newfoundland with beauty and joy and resilience. We will find the hope and humour and song amongst the despair, as our ancestors have done for centuries before us. Our essence is so much more than what we've lost. We can teach our children about our culture through our songs, and we can make them proud to call this place home. And more than that, we can bring our music around the world, as much as we will bring the world to us! *That* is what Festival 500 is.

Choirs from ten countries will visit, she says. From England, France, Ukraine, the United States, Africa. Children's choirs and adult choirs, performing all over the city. The festival will conclude with a four-hundred-voice adult choir performing Orff's *Carmina Burana*.

You women, Doreen concludes, will be such an important part of this experience for our visiting choristers. We need *you* to give them a warm place to sleep at night. Feed them, show them what we as Newfoundlanders can give them. Now! She claps her hands together. There is a table at the front of the room where you can put your names in the schedules and indicate how many people you are able to host, once you consider the size of your home, and the size of your vehicles, what you can afford to feed them, all of those logistics. Financial support will be provided. She lays her hand on her chest and closes her eyes. From the bottom of my heart, thank you.

As I mingle with the other women, my fear of being judged slips away. I feel myself relax. I feel accepted. I feel relieved.

As I leave the building that evening, Doreen takes both of my hands in hers, as she does to every woman leaving. She looks deep into my eyes. Thank you for being here, Élodie, she says. I know what you bring to this community, all of the gorgeous little girls you inspire through your own love of music and movement. We are truly blessed to have you. I hope you know that. I squeeze her hand in return.

The air feels fresh and cool on my cheeks as I step outside. I looked forward to telling Lulu about it when I get home.

I approach her bedroom and knock softly. No answer. I lean my ear against the door. I think about going downstairs to pour a drink. Old habits die hard, as they say. Instead, I walk to my bedroom and change into my nightgown. I take my time washing and moisturizing my face, the rosewater my sister brought from Paris seeping into my skin, leaving it feeling dewy. I haven't cared for myself this way in a long time.

LULU

Maman thrives when hosting. Humming and dancing throughout the house, deep side bends and stretches, pirouettes and pliés and arabesques. Incredible form for any age, let alone hers. Every now and then, she stops to stroke "Clair de lune" on the piano keys. Slowly. Day by day the notes became a little smoother, a little faster in tempo. It was one of the first pieces she'd learned to play as a girl.

Women from around the world occupy the spare bedrooms that haven't been slept in for years. Bedrooms that would've once been for the nannies and housekeepers, I guess.

Maman is a different person having actual people to care for instead of just plants and animals and hearkened spirits. She scrubs the floors and the walls, polishes the wood, shines the silverware, washes the linens and hangs them outside so they "smell like sunshine." She gets up at 5 a.m. to make breakfast. Strong, hot European coffee, and sugar cubes in a bowl. Cream in a little jug, fresh-baked buttery croissants with jam made from the strawberries growing in the backyard and the rhubarb growing in the basement. All of it laid out on the long dining-room table adorned with a crisp, white tablecloth trimmed with Victorian lace. I can't help thinking, *She's a Disney princess again.*

She drives her guests from venue to venue. The Anglican cathedral to the Roman Catholic basilica to Gower Street United. She comes home after her chauffeuring singing the songs they performed.

In between rehearsals and performances, she drives them around town, sometimes to watch the sun rise on Signal Hill, or the moon rise on Signal Hill, sometimes to wander down the pathways or just explore the infinite corners and nooks and views.

With more time with the house to myself, I've managed to make a friend. A dude in my biology class, Jared, who wants more than friendship but knows I don't. He plays in a band and wants to make movies. We talk about Camus. Sometimes we make out. Sometimes I feel guilty because, in a way, I'm only passing the time with him until it's time for me to leave. But he knows I don't want to be more than friends, so . . . I think that's okay?

The women do their vocal warm-ups in the foyer before they go to rehearsals. The walls vibrate with song. The house feels happy.

Maybe better than anything else, the singing has suffocated the fucking crow caws.

One late August evening in '97, years after Maman's first meeting with Doreen, when the last chorister has been driven to the airport, Maman and I sit side by side in the backyard swing.

Lulu. She leans close. I want to tell you a secret. Don't laugh at me, but . . . I feel there are roses blooming inside my chest. She giggles.

I roll my eyes dramatically at her, because that's my job. In that moment she feels especially dear to me. Childlike, but strong.

I mean, oh my God, Mom, that's incredibly dorky, I say, nudging her. But I'm glad you feel like that. You deserve to feel that way. She even smells like a botanical garden. Her cheeks have colour. I worry about what will happen now that everyone is gone and the house is empty again.

Lulu. She sits up straight. Squeezes my knee. Turns her face towards mine and takes my cheeks in her hands. When Papa left, I know it was extremely . . . She looks down at the ground. For that, she says, I am deeply regretful. Please know that you are my greatest love. I did not learn to love fully until you were born. Over the years, you have opened my heart so that now, finally, it can bloom into a rose.

I squirm inside. Over the years I've built up a pretty thick skin. I'm not comfortable with mushy stuff. But I stay there, my body turned to face hers, and we hug. I let myself become heavy in her arms, sinking my cheek into the back of her shoulders, just as I did when I was a toddler, just as I'd wanted to do so desperately so many times when Papa left.

You saved my life, she says, rubbing my back. Now, she gently pulls away and adjusts her shoulders backwards and does the same to mine. Book your plane ticket, s'il te plaît. You are destined to be a dancer. She tilts her chin outwards, pride radiating outwards, her eyes shining.

But what about the money?

Don't worry about the money. We have a donor who wishes to remain anonymous.

Is it . . . my father?

Ah . . . my darling . . . non . . .

Have you . . . ever been in touch with him? At all?

Maman looks down and shakes her head and my guts sink.

Me neither. He has never, ever been in touch.

Our shared abandonment is still raw to the touch. Unspoken about for years.

I change the subject. Will you be okay here on your own? If I go?

Oui, she says, relieved. I have friends now! We are planning for next year's event. This was so successful it's going to become an ongoing festival, each year! Isn't it wonderful? To be a part of something new and beloved? That you've built with other people?

Are you going to stop shopping? I worry about your finances. Tension assaults the atmosphere.

She only chuckles. Oui. I think the house is full enough now.

Are you going to get rid of the fucking crow?

She singsongs, Brandon Lee will leave when he is ready! Now, go. She hands me her credit card. Book your ticket.

I hug her long and hard. Thank you, Maman. Je t'aime.

I climb the stairs, the soft green shag carpet under my feet feeling like clouds.

Then the agent on the phone tells me the card is declined.

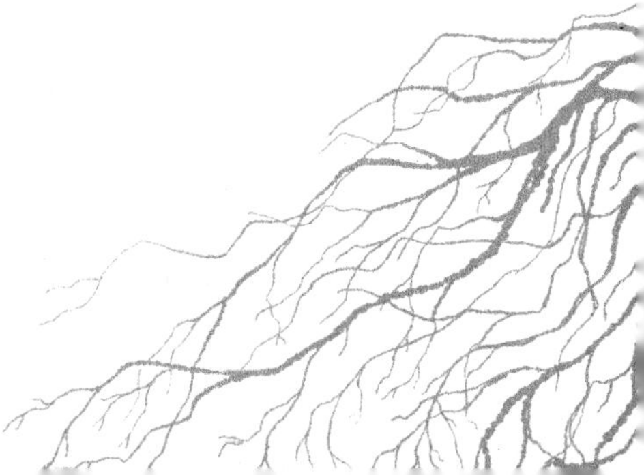

HOMEMADE BREAD

Fred Whelan sits on his favourite stump in the woods, the white of his priest's collar hanging out of the black, shooting empty Coke cans with a pellet gun. He is about ten minutes outside of Lewisporte, just off the highway, the tabernacle in plain view. He's been going there almost every night, to try to relax and bring on sleep. He'll light a fire, boil water, make a cuppa, plop a drop o' rum into it, aim the .22 calibre at the tins and try to sharpen his focus enough to make ping after ping. The impact of the shots injects Fred with an adrenaline surge and a sense of accomplishment. When he misses the shots—sure, what odds—no one's on hand to call him down to the dirt. But that doesn't mean his father's voice isn't still audible in his mind, barking, Sure yer nudding but a goddamn little girl!

Fred often brings a transistor radio. Settles it amongst the twigs and moss and cranks it as loud as it'll go. The signal is crackly, but he can pick out the voice of radio host and politician Joey Smallwood, broadcasting from his office on Circular Road in St. John's. Sometimes Fred speaks, sometimes shouts the words into the woods in between shots. He has heard so many of Smallwood's proclamations, he could have been his speechwriter:

> Our magnificent and diverse geography, our successes and enduring potential of our economy, the chronicle of the great accomplishments, individual and collective, in our history and our ability to imagine, entertain and teach through story in the tall tales of our folklore . . .

Smallwood's words feel like a hot Jiggs' Dinner under the nose of the starved beggars. Comforting. Sustaining. Nourishing. Fred hasn't felt this kind of optimism for the future since his mother's after-school sandwiches. Soft, white, homemade bread. Juicy tomatoes if they could be had. Crisp iceberg lettuce. Fat slices of bologna. Lots of mayo. Fred would sink his teeth into the mouth pillow, let the juice of the tomato and the tang of the mayo soak his taste buds and feel his mother's love warm his shoulders. Afterwards, in the quiet of their backyard, before his father came home from work, he'd lie on his back and just stare up in wonder at the white clouds against the blue sky, fluffy like the bread of his sandwich.

When his father came home, the blue always turned grey, even if there was no change in the weather. The screen door always fought for its life as he'd bound into the house. The thunder rolls. Whas 'e at out dere? Starin' up at the sky again, like a faggot?

It was the worst thing he could be called. He scrambles to his feet, thinking about little Sharon Brown sitting at her desk that day, her pretty hands neatly folded in front of her, her perfect blonde plait straight down her back, the sweet smile she gave Fred as she passed him her extra pencil. He thinks about little Sharon Brown thinking that he's a faggot, and his heart falls into his guts.

Smallwood reminds him of Father Murphy, who'd become a

confidant of his mother's after the black eyes came. Sometimes she'd bring Fred into the confession booth with her.

Bless me, Father, for I have sinned. I have not fulfilled the expectations of my father.

The church will save you, Fred, if you let it.

Little Sharon Brown lived in Lewisporte until middle school. Sometimes, she'd join Fred for his after-school sandwich.

Here, she said, my mother sent cookies. The pairing of their mothers' snacks, them sitting together at a kitchen table, warmed Fred's shoulders, and it was all he wanted the future to be.

We'll write, promise me we'll write, said little Sharon Brown, about to climb into her family's Cadillac, her cheeks wet, her big blue eyes sparkling swimming pools. The Newfoundland Bible belt was just starting to spawn in 1939, so it was only a matter of time before her paternal parent, a Pentecostal pastor, would move them on to another town.

The letters continued for about a year after she left. Then . . . nothing.

The church will save you, Fred, if you let it.

He waited five years until he joined the ministry. Five years since the letters stopped.

Father Murphy was a guiding force during Fred's time in the ministry. Heavy hands on Fred's shoulders. Close, long hugs. A big finger, dragging the base of a cross down and across Fred's chest. It was better than his own father's You're not worth my piss, you're not. When his mother got sick, and lost her battle, Father Murphy and the congregation were all Fred had.

I'm always with you, Fred, she had said, holding Fred's hand, her grasp weak, her fingers as light as paper, her eyes half-closed, closing, closing, until her spirit floated through the window and into the white clouds.

That was the day the visits to the woods began. Where he could be alone, smell nature, look at the clouds without interruption.

But even there, the demons found him.

Fred consumed Smallwood's words. Scrutinized the newsreels as he stacked the hymn books after mass, choking on the smell of the books, bile rising in his throat just looking at the pews. He knew of the little man's broadcasting empire, his fervent speaking style—bark of a car salesman, charisma of a Broadway producer. He grinned and shook hands with the prime minister of Canada. The Great Depression had sunk their province into a dismal economic state, the streets of St. John's peppered with youngsters in rags, starved half to death. Houses that looked like shacks. The war gave temporary reprieve, but after it ended and the Americans left, people feared for the future. News broadcasters madly typed stories for his newspaper, recorded episodes of his radio program, *The Barrelman*. Smallwood speaks in staccato. His intonation cracks and snaps.

> It is in our little Dominion's best interest to join the great country of Canada! This union will bring economic prosperity to Newfoundland! *Free* us from the effects of the *Great* De*pression*! Do *not* be fooled. Our economy has been *crushed* by this dismal time in history. Col*lapsed*. An accordion, *slammed* shut. *Silenced*. We are small. But We. Are. MIGHTY! We *can* rebound. We *will* rebound. And Canada? *Is* the answer!

Hope Springs Eternal.

The vote for confederation was close: 77,869 against 71,464.

Ruralites benefitted from the union. The promise of cash advances from Canada put dollar signs and possibility in their eyes.

Fred was no different. Alone in the woods, he sometimes cracked the spine on some of his mother's old books. Alexander Pope's "An Essay on Man" was in regular rotation: *Know then thyself, presume not God to scan; The proper study of mankind is man.* Enough sitting in the woods, shooting tin cans.

He buys a ticket for the Newfoundland Railway, known by locals as the Newfie Bullet—a rich irony as the train sludges along at slug speed. Fred slinks into a seat near the front of the car and drops his duffel bag at his feet. The one useful thing his father left him when he left them. The .22 calibre is well disguised amongst clothes. The train sputters into motion and Fred's thoughts start to chug.

The train speeds up as it chugs outside of town and reaches countryside. The rocks and the bogs and the ponds and trees blur together in broad paint strokes of nothing and of everything, and Fred's thoughts roll at an unhealthy pace.

You're not worth my piss, you're not.

The church will save you, Fred, if you let it.

We'll write, promise me, we'll write.

I'll always be with you, Fred. Even after I'm gone, I'll always be with you.

It is in our little Dominion's best interest to join Canada.

The voices become a brash cacophony of sound, thrashing around in his skull. Questions course through his veins, and his thyroid throbs and thumps in his ears.

Why wasn't I worth your piss? Your worthless, diseased, shitty piss?

How has the church saved me? What has my life been? Days upon days of sitting within suffocating walls, wearing stiff clothes, never being able to express my feelings, behaving a certain way . . . How has the church saved me?

Why did I stop getting letters from you? What did I do? I loved you. I still do. You abandoned me.

How will you always be with me? You're gone. Dead in the ground. Left me alone here. You abandoned me.

They lied. All of them. Everyone lies. No one, no thing, is sacred.

The hurt and fury bump around inside his chest cavity like a dropped basketball, bouncing off his rib cage, clunking into his guts and his heart, rebounding off the back of his throat. From head to toe he aches with rage, grief, rejection, neglect, yet . . . he wants everything he lost and everything he never had. A father. A mother. A lover. Peace.

The train chugs to the station on Water Street, in St. John's, finally. The harbour smells of fish and coal from the city's heating source. His duffel bag flung over his shoulder, Fred walks until he finds a market. The second he's through the door, a bin of blood-red tomatoes stares him in the face. He holds one in his hand. Closes his eyes. The cool skin is as smooth as a skimming rock. The feel of it against the pads of his fingers takes the rage down a notch. The bread is just over to the left, the bologna to the right. He goes straight for the homemade loaf of white, remembering that during the Depression his mother refused to use the whole wheat flour that was healthier because it was given out on the dole. The buttery crust shines under the lighting, and the density is cloud-like. The bread smells of comfort.

Bread, bologna, tomato, a small jar of mayo. T'ree dollars, says the laddio in the newsboy cap.

Outside, sitting on a bench next to the door, Fred pulls a pocket knife from his jacket and lays his food out on his lap. Tears the bread apart. Slices the tomato and the bologna. Goops mayonnaise onto the soft loaf. Juice soaks his pants, but he does not care. He is ravenous and can only think of his teeth sinking into the sandwich. He closes his eyes, and the sandwich becomes a part of him. He sucks in the juice of the tomato and the salt of the bologna and the tartness of the mayo like a vampire draining blood from a body. The sandwich makes him immortal. He licks dabs of mayonnaise off the tips of his fingers as he finishes the meal. He packs the remaining bread, bologna and mayo into the duffel bag, careful when unzipping it, lest anyone catch a glimpse of the .22 calibre. He stands, sweeps the crumbs from his lap and soldiers forth.

The streets in St. John's smell of horse manure. On Duckworth Street, lads dart across the roads, jumping onto and off of cable cars. Fred trudges up Garrison Hill, towards the Roman Catholic basilica, his steps slow but deliberate. He still tastes the salt from the bologna on the back of his tongue, and he desperately wants rum. If God really existed, there would be rum.

In his mind, he hears Smallwood's voice, broadcasting a signal just for him.

Come here, my son. Here is your new hope, right here in St. John's. You are a part of the New Newfoundland. You *will* help *bring us* for*ward. The staccato syllable spat out is a call to arms.*

Fred tromps through Georgestown until Smallwood's home and offices on Circular Road is in clear view. Its sharp window peaks looking like angry eyebrows. Its height ominous against the grey clouds in the April sky. The sight of it does not make Fred feel the way he thought he would feel. He imagines the premier, sitting at his desk behind that front top window—Fred has seen the newspaper photos of him standing in the office, smiling, confident, his thick black glasses matching the desk. Fred imagines him there, furiously jabbing the typewriter keys, guiding his people to a greener future with his charismatic words and his messages of hope and confidence. And the optimism Fred felt in the past flushes into anger. You're not worth my piss, you're not. The church will guide you, if you let it. Poison. No man had ever given Fred real hope. The weight of the church presses on his shoulders, its gargantuan stone walls, its heavy wooden doors, the poisonous air inside of it, his father and Father Murphy sitting in its pews, threatening to swallow him up.

Smallwood is no different. This Colonial Monstrosity that is Canada House is no different.

His pace quickens as he approaches the doors, and with his fingers he feels the bones of the .22 calibre underneath its skin of clothes and duffel bag. Without even seeing him, Fred knows Smallwood is inside, he feels the little man's sharp energy, the same barking bite that ejaculated through the radio waves. The same bark his father had when he came home from work. The front door is but twenty feet away, and Fred's tunnel vision on its handle is tack sharp.

Until he hears a door creak open to the left, around the side of the house. He freezes in his tracks. Allows his vision to widen to survey the scene. He senses it's a woman before he even sees her. She turns the corner of the house carrying a mop and pail in one hand and two dusters in the other. She is looking at the ground until a crow caws and she looks to the sky, and Fred is stabbed in the heart at the sight of her face. It has been ten years—a long ten years but only ten years—and her face is the same. Sharon. His full body softens. His expression melts, from steely and emotionless to fearful and sad. His heart throbs, not with fury, but something else. Pain. Regret. Love.

Her gaze drops from the sky straight to Fred and she freezes. Drops the pail and they are both frozen in their tracks. Fred is finally able to yank one foot out of the invisible wet concrete it's been stuck in and take one step in the right direction. The step turns into a gait and Sharon has dropped the rest of her items and she's running and they throw their arms around each other and she lays her cheek onto his chest and Fred's heart pounds so loud that he's almost embarrassed. She squeezes him tighter.

Fred lifts his face to a place in the sky that is brightening. A blue patch, with white clouds the texture of his mother's homemade bread. He is a child again, lying on his back on the grass. The sun warms Fred's face.

MIDNIGHT TOAST

One day you will ask me which is more important?
My life or yours?
I will say mine and you will walk away
not knowing that you are my life.
—Khalil Gibran

Hey, man, you believe in ghosts? Voice sedated, like soft jazz, the flowy-haired hippy from the apartment next door jangles her keys from her messenger bag and flips her auburn locks away from her eye.

Ben is a deer in headlights. He's seen her around. In the hazy smoke of the student centre on campus, only half-real. Come and go from the main part of the house as he's come and gone from the apartment around the side and up the stairs. He is embarrassingly heart eyed over her aura—floaty, half-present, there in body but part of her eternally blowing around with the autumn leaves and beyond, swirling with the cloud matter, ethereal.

But they've never exchanged words. He has always been too intimidated to make eye contact.

No, he says. But one day a fella over there—he nods towards Fleming Street, diagonal across the road—goes, Ya ever notice whenever there's a ghost around, it smells like bacon?

Well, now. She purses her lips and looks sideways, coy, her gaze towards the clouds and then right at him. I've never heard of that before. She sniffs the air, her adorable small nose scrunching like a squirrel's. I don't smell bacon. Do you smell bacon?

He can only shake his head. She turns the key. Her white go-go boots all but glow under the December sun. Magical, electric-guitar snowflakes, fused with her being, carrying her around town.

I'm Delia, by the way, she says.

Ben. I'm Ben.

God. Her eyes. Lavender? Do lavender eyes exist?

Ben. We're havin' a New Year's party on Friday. Bunch of folks from the Folklore Department, she says. Musicians. It'll be groovy. Come by if you're free.

She pushes the door open and sends a coy, flirtatious smile his way. Waves, her fingers fanning out before she clasps a fist and vanishes through the door.

Did that just happen?

He makes his way up the fire-escape steps, towards their apartment. Inside, Annie sits at the kitchen table, her glasses on the end of her nose, leaning over a biology textbook. As usual. Lab notes spread all over the table, some of them on the floor. She looks up briefly. Hi. Before looking at the notes, frowning.

He presses the button on the toaster. Midnight toast. They've been doing it every Thursday night since they moved into the apartment nearly a year ago. What once felt warm and nurturing now feels like just an action.

Annie and Ben met at the Alice Cooper concert at the Thomson Student Centre. Packed, shoulder to shoulder, the crowd thrashing together like a rogue wave. Ben banged into Annie's shoulder, spilling beer all over her. He stiffened, anticipating a smack or a shove or a hard stare.

His inferiority complex runs deep. Constant requests to do more, more, more from his father. He felt like nothing more than a carbon copy. A reproduction. For his first junior high dance ever, he had taken great care selecting his outfit. He found a checkered blazer—bright-red and black—at the thrift shop in town. Bright-red bowtie. Matching shoes. The night came, and he readied himself, excited to present a piece of his true essence to the world.

The look on his father's face when he entered the living room was a hack to his soul.

My Jesus, sure ya looks like a fuckin' clown.

Ben was just shitbaked enough to even go to a dance in the first place, let alone be insulted by the one he should idolize. The dig planted a seed that sprouted into an inferiority complex that bloomed over and over again throughout Ben's life. He withdrew emotionally from his girlfriends, leaving them in a puddle of what-just-happened? His relationships always started the same, full of hope, adoration, romance. He would shower them with affection, his eyes sparkling at how they made him feel, and then . . . weeks would pass, months if it was really special, years in one case, until his father's words from that fateful day would creep from his subconscious into his conscience and he'd flatline. Go steely and withdraw. Stop trying. It happened over and over again. Hunky-dory, until the thought hit him, as it always did eventually: *They're only going to realize I'm a clown.*

Until Annie. Things felt different with Annie.

You got me all wet! She laughed, that night at the Alice Cooper show. The relief nearly turned *him* to a puddle of what-just-happened?

Oh shit, I'm so sorry. I'll get you another one.

He was tingly from head to toe.

They were glued at the hip for the rest of the night. After the show, they strolled downtown together, eventually ending up sitting on the grass in the middle of a ring of trees in Bannerman Park.

So, what do you be at all the time, Annie?

Well, I play volleyball. I go to classes. I'm doing a science degree. What about you?

He'd applied to university, and they made him take a course in how to speak proper English: it meant that you couldn't even *speak* well enough yet to be in university. He didn't even have to say anything for Annie to energetically sense the chop to his already-fragile confidence. She looked at him, soft and sympathetic, hopeful and expectant, not a hint of pity. And his insides softened.

Oh, I'm . . . still just trying to figure it out. Workin' at Sobeys now, the one at the mall. He was conscious of his accent, trying to tame it from taking over.

Oh! Maybe that's where I've seen you before. Rolling the baskets through the conveyer belt with the flappy doors for people to pick up. Dad and I love that one.

You and your dad close?

Best buds.

Oh yeah?

Yeah. She leaned her head on his shoulder and scooched closer to him on the grass. What about you? Are you close with your parents?

Somehow, it all spilled out of him that night. How he felt pressure to make them proud. First generation who could possibly go to university. Be educated, said Mom. Dad wanted him to stay home and carry on with the fishing trade. Mom worked at the plant, encouraged him to take the free tuition granted by Smallwood.

We're just so good as the rest of 'em, she had said, squeezing his shoulders, looking into his eyes. You got to take advantage of the opportunities you got. We never 'ad that.

His mother's encouragement warmed him, made him feel valued. And so, despite Fadder's grumbles, off he went to St. John's. Found a spot in the apartment with a buddy who also wanted to do more with his life.

It was the first time he'd spoken about his feelings to another living soul.

Did you go to the student protests? she said, just before dawn.

Oh yeah, he said. Front and centre.

It was only the highlight of his life. He'd never felt more alive. In opposition to mandatory student fees, about fifteen hundred students gathered on campus in the Thomson centre, storming the Arts and Admin building, setting up "revolutionary headquarters" in the Little Theatre. They camped there for three nights. There were musical performances, an organized food service. It was a community of oneness, a group fighting peacefully for equality.

Ben was kicked out of the university shortly after the occupation ended. He couldn't keep his grades up.

I was there, too, Annie said. Imagine, we could've met then.

Mmm.

We weren't meant to meet until now, I guess.

They lay on the grass, fingers interlaced, until the sun came up.

Ben's buddy moved out of the apartment a few months after that. He'd met up with a group of musicians.

It's just easier to fit in jams if we're livin' together. You get it, right, man? We cool?

Oh yeah. No problem. *I'll just pay the full rent myself, I guess.*

I think we could be roomies, couldn't we? Annie's eyes had sparkled up at him and warmed his insides. They'd only been together for three months, but it could've been thirty years. She felt, strangely, like the home he never knew. He didn't know if he should trust it but somehow, he did.

For months, they lived in peace and harmony. He'd bring home the groceries, she'd do the dishes. They took turns cooking. She'd study, he'd play hockey with the boys. In the evenings they'd settle in to watch *Get Smart* or *Doctor Who* or *Gilligan's Island* reruns on her father's old Sony TV. It was a comfortable, stable existence.

But as he continued to work at Sobey's, and nothing more, the air between them seemed to stiffen.

So . . . any thoughts about reapplying? she asked one day, over Hunt's canned spaghetti and a side garden salad with iceberg lettuce and chunks of tomato, drenched in Kraft Thousand Island Dressing.

He rubbed the back of his neck. I just . . . I don't know what to do. I don't want to be a teacher. Don't want to do what I went in for.

The threat of disapproval began to rise in him, the familiar sick feeling more dreadful than usual. Was he becoming too dependent on her?

That's okay, you'll figure it out. She squeezed his shoulder, but he felt the air change. The threat of resentment.

She became more focused on her studies.

One day about a month ago, after he'd met her for lunch between classes at the Spanish Cafe, he kissed her goodbye and hung around for a while. Wandered around campus. Found himself in the Thomson Student Centre. Walked through the doors into the realm of peacoats and marijuana smoke. Droopy eyelidded arts students.

Hey, man. You look a little lost, said a tall, slim, giraffe-necked stoner wearing a Joe Cocker baseball tee.

Just . . . checkin' the place out.

It's good, it's all good, man. Hey, Dr. Music's playin' here next week.

Holy shit, no way.

I do say, my man. I do say.

Ben walked to work that day on a cloud. The beginning of transcendence, although he didn't recognize it as that at the time. A little piece of the next version of himself had been presented as he stepped through the Thomson centre vestibule, into the outside world, into the dreamlike vapour of academic rebellion.

Annie crunches the toast Ben lays in front of her.

So just now, he says, I ran into the woman who lives next door. She invited us to a New Year's party.

Oh? Annie looks up. And you . . . wanna go?

Yeah . . . I think I do.

Well . . . the biology department head is having a party too. He lives further down on Circular. Towards the stadium.

In the rich end, ha.

We're in the rich end, Ben.

Well, yeah . . . but the servants' quarters is just across the road. We're close enough.

Well . . . maybe we can do both?

Ben's gut sinks. He doesn't want to go to the biology party. Who needs to feel stupid? He's spent most of his life feeling that way. But looking at Annie, sitting there with her books open, hair mussed, her glasses slipping down her nose . . . he still feels that same warmth of home and he yearns for it, the desperation to hang on. Acceptance. Possibility. Future. He wants it more than anything.

What if their love affair is ending? If it is, he doesn't yet recognize his feelings as denial. The atmosphere around him carries the energies of those who came before and of those who will come after, knowing things he himself doesn't yet know. Every pulse in their every vein, every nuance of their every emotion, every intention of genuine feelings that's been shrouded by perceived manipulation, suffocating beautiful connections throughout time, floats in the air around him. Even if Ben doesn't recognize that his love for Annie is actually just denial, the walls know the truth, waiting to seep through his skin when the time is right.

Beyond the walls, on New Year's Eve, like every New Year's Eve, in every house, under every sky of fireworks, the night holds menace and melancholy. With such high expectations for joy, how can it not set you up for failure? On New Year's Eve, all the sadness of the world seems to well up in the air and burst out at the stroke of midnight. Every pent-up emotion, every fear, every suspicion gets yelled out, released in the guise of a HAPPY NEW YEAR!

Like a good boy, Ben has zipped his khakis and tucked his polo shirt into his pants for the biology mixer. He looks at his watch and schedules in his mind how much time exactly he has to turn into a pumpkin. It's 8 p.m. Surely, they won't have to stay there beyond three hours? Surely, they'll be back where they belong before midnight?

Ben, she says, leading him towards a tall, broad-shouldered man wearing a striped wool turtleneck and tan cords. This is Professor Hawke, my thesis supervisor.

Hawke holds out his hand to shake Ben's. His sturdy shake and intense eye are intended to make Ben feel threatened. It works.

Pleased to meet you, sir. You're a lucky man, with such a gorgeous young genius by your side, Hawke says.

Yes, sir. He shakes his hand right back, staring into his eyes despite wanting to disintegrate but simultaneously feeling his jealousy bubble deep, desperately trying to suppress it. I am indeed lucky. *When will she realize I'm not good enough? Maybe tonight.*

As Annie mingles into the crowd, excited to see her classmates, pouring herself a generous glass of Mateus, her attempts to integrate Ben into the group melt away. Ben checks his watch regularly. To him, the conversation sounds like the murmels and warbles of Charlie Brown's teacher. At nine fifteen he gently places a hand on the small of her back. Just going to the washroom, he whispers in her ear.

Zipping his fly, he thinks, *She won't notice if I slip away for a bit.* He washes his hands and regards himself in the mirror. Stretches his mouth down, tilts back his head to make sure there's no snot. There is a little one. He dabs it away with his index finger. Medium-brown hair. Straight. Cut neat. Blue eyes. Light scruff. Could never quite achieve a smooth shave. Lips, not too thin, not impressively full either. Chin, not weak, but not John Wayne strong. There's nothing particularly wrong with his looks. He wouldn't consider himself handsome either. He's just a bay boy, that's all. Exiting the bathroom, he weaves himself through the small house, packed with the science-minded, babbling with fervour, the intensity in the room something outside of Ben. He eyeballs Annie, absorbed in whatever Hawke is gesticulating about. He heads towards the front door, shucks his coat over his shoulders, clicks the doorknob and nips out into the crisp, mysterious night. Strides down Circular. When he approaches the house, he can already hear the bass thump from the speakers. The windows are dark, but red-and-blue party lights dance into the night.

The entire house seems to throb, harder and harder into his eardrums and his heart with each step closer. When he pushes the front door open and steps inside, it's as if he has been suctioned through a tunnel to a different level of existence. The thudding speakers, the music, the voices, the smoke, the lights . . . The air alone makes him feel high.

Ben!

Delia.

She seems to float towards him, a Stevie Nicks slash Brigitte Bardot vibe, wearing a long, floral, translucent kimono. The go-go boots, a body-hugging black minidress—sleeveless with a mock turtleneck—giant, thick silver-hoop earrings. Lilac and silver cat eyes. She shimmers. Her arms outstretched, fluid, she sways from side to side until she reaches him. Her scent dives into his nostrils, swims up into his brain, front crawls and backstrokes around in his mind. She wraps her arms around his neck and pulls him in. Her hair smells like lavender.

I'm so glad you came! Here, let me take your coat. She holds out her arms while he shrugs it off his shoulders. He scans the lavish foyer. She tosses his coat at the foot of the stairs, nonchalant, and he glances at it there, on the floor, surprised at the casual discard. She throws her head back to release the most mellifluous laughter he has ever heard. You'll find it again if you're meant to. She winks. Maybe it's the old coat of an old you. She lays a hand on his shoulder. Lemme give you the tour . . .

The entrance hall is opulently shabby. Shaggy olive-green carpet. A dripping crystal chandelier hanging over the curved staircase splashes occasional tiny rainbows on the wall when the light hits the right way, creating a light spectrum when it's meant to appear. At the foot of the staircase, a giant, gold-gilded mirror. Annie leads him to it. What do you see in there, Ben?

He blinks twice, fast, seeing a man who differed from the mediocre. Someone altogether different from the reflection he saw at the party. Shrouded in the red-and-blue lights, the rainbows—tiny prisms of prospective partners and potentials bursting into existence out of seemingly nowhere, exploding, settling gently onto his shoulders, landing on his eyelashes. Seeping into his skin. He can't quite believe what he's seeing and feeling, here, in the company of these particular people, in this particular place.

He feels Delia watching him, watching himself. Senses her hand on his arm. He looks down, her moonstone ring glistening under the lights. She nods towards the kitchen. Come on back here, I'll fix you up with a libation or two. She turns, moving like an apparition down the hallway, her kimono billowing out from her sides, her curls illuminated. The people around her wear fur hats shaped like helmets. Long, paisley-patterned dresses and peasant blouses. Miniskirts and go-go boots. Drapey scarves. Hoop earrings. Bell bottoms, bell sleeves, halter necks and platforms. Girls who shop at London, New York, Paris on Water Street.

Carnaby Street–style, a host of lengths, sleeves, colours and fabrics on parade.

What's your poison?

Uhh, just a beer if you've got it?

You betcha. She hands him a Blue Star stubby. The label reads *The Star of Newfoundland*. Come and meet some new people.

He follows her into the living slash dining room area. His head tilts backwards as he takes in the twelve-foot ceilings, floor to ceiling covered in velvet wallpaper. He runs a hand along the wall and feels the softness on his fingertips. The air, thick with marijuana smoke, people dancing and singing, hands running up and down bodies . . . Ben needs another beer or two before he can settle in here.

Come check out the second-floor vibe. Delia nods towards the stairs, taking his hand, leading him back out to the foyer. She pauses at the mirror. See you two later, she says, kissing the glass before stepping up the stairs. The bedrooms are all open, the music much quieter. People sit with guitars, strumming, scrawling a few words on paper, notes on a staff. Some noodle and pluck mindlessly while chatting with another person or two. Some are more intent on their work. People sit cross-legged, against a wall, or lie dreamily on a bed . . . The second floor is calmly ignited with a party buzz that's more subdued than the first floor. Scanning the rooms, a glow in his core, Ben notices the tall guy with the Joe Cocker T-shirt he met at the TSC recently. They pass a room with a steep-slanted A-frame ceiling, red wallpaper, dark wood floors.

You know Smallwood used to live and work here, right? Delia leans close to Ben's ear.

No, I didn't, actually. Ben feels a prickle at the back of his neck. Ghosts.

It wasn't that long ago he moved out actually. The Canadian government acquired this place in '41, and Smallwood's offices and residence were here from '49 to '60.

Her fingers graze along the ornate walls, decorated with white velvet curls against a red-silk background. How many bigwigs had run their fingers across the paper? In the main bathroom across the hall there, she says, there's Toulouse wallpaper that Smallwood brought back from Paris.

Ben imagines Smallwood pacing in his bedroom in his underwear, dreaming up the speeches he'd bark through the radio waves, in front of the swarms of supporters and the throngs of angry students who didn't trust him. What would he have seen in the mirror at the foot of the stairs?

This hallway here? Delia says. This leads to your apartment. Bet you didn't know that.

Huh. Ben pictures their space and realizes now, only now, where the hobbit-size door in the back of their bedroom leads. They'd noticed it, wondered what was inside. It was locked. They'd talked about breaking it open, looking inside. It's probably just storage, Annie said. But something about it felt foreboding.

Holy shit, he says.

Yeah. I know. Delia winks.

Ben scans the space, the rooms, the hallways, the bright-red carpet on the floors, trying to imagine how the different sections of the house fit together.

Time for the bottom-floor tour now. She laces her fingers into Ben's. As they head back to the stairs, the tall dude from the TSC intersects them.

James, my friend! Delia raises her arm in the air, and she and James lace fingers. We're heading to the basement. You in?

You know it. James nods towards Ben. Smiles. Hey, man, he says, droopy eyed, good to see ya again.

They glide down the steps, wordlessly, and a couple other select people seem to follow their trail to another door behind the steps. Delia jimmies it open, and they descend to another level, right in the house's bowels. She leads them through a wine cellar.

We're in what would've been the servants' quarters, she says. She opens another short door, and behind it is what seems like a crawl space. The ceilings, sloped, too low to stand in. Purply-blue scarves balloon from the Gyproc, a couple of lava lamps light the space. Four of them sit on the floor. The space can hold no more. James rolls a joint.

Ben, Delia says, you know James already, apparently. This is Julianna. She points to the third person who's followed them to the basement.

Hey, buddy, nice to meet ya, says Julianna.

Good to be here with ya, man, says James.

Ben feels that they mean it. There are no pretenses here. Only sincerity. Genuine interest.

Ya know what? Delia puts a hand on James's hand. We're on the cusp of a new year here. Hell, a new decade. The '70s, baby! I think we should absorb something even more "of the earth" than grass.

Shrooms? James's droopy smile lifts slightly.

Only if . . . we're all groovy with that?

Ben has never done shrooms, but something about this collection of people tells him that he should.

They all agree and Delia produces a teak-wood box she has tucked around the corner, with brown bark-like pieces inside. She sprinkles a little in everyone's hand.

Ready? She makes eye contact with everyone in the circle. Go.

Ben has to take an extra swig from the stubby to get the dry flakes down.

Julianna asks Ben where he works and he says Sobeys. Tells her his girlfriend is doing biology and Julianna perks at this bit of news. She's doing biology as well and knows Annie.

She's good, she's good. We're in a couple of classes together.

Yeah, before I got here, I was at a party with a bunch of those folks. How come you weren't there?

Ah, I was earlier, but knew this one would be the better spot to end the night. She nods, smug.

I . . . really didn't feel like I fit in there.

Yeah . . . the whole science-arts divide, hey, man? James nods. You're a liberal arts dude, I can tell.

You think?

I know.

I can see it, too. Delia lays a hand on his shoulder. You've got stories inside you.

Maybe you're a writer, says Julianna. Or a folklorist. You should do a folklore course.

Well, though . . . the whole science-arts-spirituality divide is a bit bullshitty if you ask me. Julianna snorts. I mean, if you know brain anatomy, every feeling is just connected to somewhere in the brain. It's complex, but once you understand it, the pain of heartache seems more controllable. Less abstract and mystical, or something. Science!

Colours become more vibrant. The purple of Delia's eyeshadow, the scarves on the ceiling . . . Julianna's red scarf, her red lips . . . a hazy, blurred, dreamlike quality.

James rakes his fingers across the cold floor. Some people say spirituality is what happens when you run out of science. Spirituality is beyond all science, space and matter.

No, the black hole is beyond all space and matter, Julianna says. Science tells us.

Hey, this is gonna sound real random, says James, but . . . does anyone smell bacon?

Ben gets a shiver on the back of his neck.

Delia bolts upright. Let's go in there. She points towards a small door behind the stairs, made of cheap, brown wood panelling.

What's in there? Ben watches the wood grains moving, rippling like water in slow motion.

Delia exchanges a smirk with Julianna and James.

You'll see. Trust us, she says. She jiggles and jimmies the door open, freeing it from its stuckness. The damp, cool air floats from the door opening, swims over his skin, wraps around his shoulders and draws him towards its mouth. He crawls towards it, trancelike and in wonder.

Just keep going. You'll know when it's time to stop, says Delia, who is right behind him.

He smells gravel. Rock and dirt. Musty, soggy space surrounding him. He digs his fingers into the soil, imagining them as a rake. He can't see much, can only sense what might be near. He keeps crawling, crawling, heart thumping, pulse pumping, prominent in his jugular.

Soon the tunnel feels more expansive. The space around him widens. He takes in a sumptuous suck of air, thick and muggy.

Okay, we can stand up now, says Delia. We're underneath the Colonial Building.

There's a lamp just over here, says James, his voice contained by the dampness in the soil. He strikes a match and lights an old lantern. Once illuminated, the tree roots are visible in the dirt walls. Languid, seemingly moving through a gelatinous clear fluid.

Ben's body feels like that, too. His shoulders droop, his arms dragging downwards, as if they might reach into and below the ground, down, down, turning him upside down into a handstand, his fingers sprouting roots, spreading into the earth, his body and legs and feet growing branches as he becomes part of the cave.

Delia whispers in an aristocratic British accent, This is where Prime Minister Sir Richard Squires hid out when the angry protestors wanted to murder him in the 1932 riot.

Yes indeed, says James in equally terrible cockney. The people were none too 'appy that the gov'nah spiked the taxes.

Julianna collapses in laughter.

Delia follows suit. The fucking colonists. Such twats.

Yew know . . . Ben chimes in . . . Proime Ministah Squires 'ad to dress like a woman to escape! Barely made it out aloive!

Yew don't SAY, James adds in, and the two guys fall on the ground, laughing until their jaws hurt.

Okay, okay . . . we must soldier on then.

Delia takes Julianna's hand, who takes Ben's hand, who takes

James's. The four of them creep through the room until they have to crouch into another crawling section.

You know, there've been dozens of secret rooms found in houses around St. John's. Buried pasts everywhere. Don't you still feel them here? Delia says.

There's definitely war bunkers, says James. Bomb shelters. This was a wartime city.

Well, there are secret spaces, unknown areas, of houses all over the city. I mean, I didn't even know this tunnel from our house existed until I'd lived there for a full year, says Delia. People find pre-war saws, old tools and soda bottles, old newspaper articles in their houses . . . We're excavating time as we move through life.

Ben feels the people who existed in and above these spaces before him, as if he were crawling outside of his own ego. He is nothing and he is everything. This is the space between science and spirituality. He is not an atom or a neuron or cells or skin or hair. He is just one part of the everything. The roots and soil around him seem to dance, groove, flow alongside their bodies. *With* their bodies.

Ben says he needs outside air, and Delia agrees and says she thinks she remembers how to get back.

She *thinks*?

Crawling back through the dirt, a sudden wave of nausea swoops through his body. His pulse quickens. He scrambles, crawling quicker, scraping at the dirt, desperate to get back to his own life. What had he been waiting for? He sees it all clearly before him. He just has to get to it. His future is in political science. History. Activism.

The nausea morphs into an inner warmth, a red-orange glow within. He is whole, he is complete.

I love you I love you I love you, don't give up on me, don't give up on me, don't give up on me.

He scrambles through the dirt until Delia reaches the small door. She slinks through. She is gone. Ben lumbers through the door that was locked. Except on the other side is not the crawl space with purple-bruise scarves. There is no Delia. He is in their apartment. Annie sits at the table—a plate of toast, two glasses of champagne.

Happy New Year! She smiles.

From next door, he hears the party cheer, Five! Four! Three! Two! One! Happy New Year!

Ben, I'm so sorry. Annie stretches her hands across the table. He sits at the table and takes her hands in his, noticing the dirt packed under his fingernails and lodged in the grooves of his knuckles. Life is full of dirt to dig through. He'd be lucky to hold her hands through it all.

She looks into his eyes. I'm so sorry if I made you feel unsafe, you stopped trusting me, or if something I said made you feel bad. I'm just so, so sorry. She picks up his hands and presses them against her cheek. I think you're wonderful. I'm sorry I made you go to the biology party.

Ben slides his hands around her shoulders, her back, and folds her into his chest. Inhales the scent of her hair, Johnson's Baby Shampoo. Tucks his nose into her. Tightens his grip. Holds her even closer, if that's possible.

There will always be politics. Annie will move into marine biology. They will advocate for change. They will fight the ghosts of the past.

He hugs Annie.

He is here. He is home.

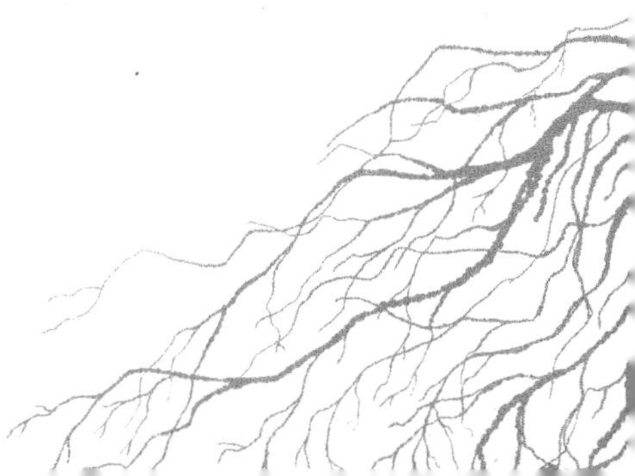

TURNS TO

a micro-novel

chapter 1

Huddling in the corner of a kitchen party, knees up to our chests, bodies leaning into each other. Hot whispers in ears. The room is full of people, yet we are the only two here.

Turns To a night walk, arm in arm, shoulder to shoulder, cheek to cheek, mazing through the downtown streets. A Strawberry Moon, rose gold, round, bright, brilliant against a dark navy-blue backdrop. The air, crispy clammy kissy on our skin.

Turns To a long, slow, melty melding of lips that don't let go until dawn.

chapter 2

Poring over pages of random books at the Peter E. On the end tables, five-dollar Guinness pints. Levi's touching. Fingers comb lightly across a butt cheek. Glimmers of newness shimmer in the spoon collection on the wood-panelled wall. Possibility. Who-knows-what-who-cares-what. Happenstance? Luck? Fluke? Fate?

Fuck it, whatever it is.

Sway our way up Long's Hill. Right across Military. Left down Bonaventure.

Turns To eight hours later. (Whoops, it only felt like two. Three, tops.)

chapter 3

A walk in the sunny woods Turns To a run in the rain. Tumble into the house. Spark the fireplace. Peel off our clothes, like wet bark off a tree, the smell of wet moss from outside still in our noses and we're lichen it. Jump under a blanket on the couch.

Limbs entwined. Spooning. Talking. Laughing.

Afternoon Turns To dusk.

What's for supper?

A brie wheel, doused in BBQ sauce, baked. A fresh baguette, bought this morning from the bakery down the road. Scoop up that hot, gooey goodness.

Dusk Turns To dark.

White wine. Electric Light Orchestra, *Out of the Blue* (1977).

Up to the second floor, the sex floor. Pillow talk. Suddenly it's 4 a.m. Laughing like school-aged kids at a slumber party.

chapter 4

Cohabitation.

Sleepovers every night now. Toast and coffee in the morning Turns To toast and bourbon at midnight. Becomes a tradition.

A pat on the ass on the way out the door for a sunrise jog Turns To a grab of the ass under the moonlight, under the sheets.

chapter 5

On go the years.

Sleepovers every night.

Every. Single. Night?

Toast and coffee in the morning still Turns To toast and bourbon at midnight.

Every. Single. Night.

chapter 6

Babies cooing. Cuddling. Can you believe we made this beautiful creature?

Another baby. Now we are four.

A third baby. This one cries more.

Five beings, one bursting family unit, in all its mayhem, love, chaos, tears.

Crying, lying, denying, rectifying.

A conversation about feelings Turns To a long, damp, teary hug and a soppy, weepy romp.

Trying.

Sleepovers every night. Midnight toast gets stale.

A conversation about feelings Turns To an argument.

Trying . . . ?

A conversation about feelings Turns To silence.

"Turn to Stone." Track one from *Out of the Blue*.

No more Strawberry Moon.

Floating in space.

Dying.

chapter 7

How does it happen that the apple of the eye, the glimmer in the gloom, the illuminator of insides now crushes them? That the magnetic force that attracts two people so strongly grows to repel them?

Untangle the ravaged, pummelled, punched, bruised heart. Don't get too angry. Well, okay, get angry, but don't stay angry. Keep it kind. Remember the love.

But it's not enough.

chapter 8

One person got mean. The other person gets mean. One person stops listening. The other person does the same.

Trust broken.

Regret. Guilt. Desolation. Despair.

Anger: a jacket for sadness.

I sat with my anger long enough until she told me her real name was grief, said C.S. Lewis.

Love is fire, destructive yet delicate.

chapter 9

Spark the fireplace. Sprinkle with kindling. Caress the flames. Poke the embers. Get it to flare. Keep the flame going.

No, no, wait—tame the flame. The fire needs to be monitored. Always. A series of inattentive moves can end in disaster. A low, even crackle—that's the sweet spot. Warm and calm and safe.

Love crackles with contradiction, ready to burn the whole house down.

chapter 10

Now it's just scattered black ash in the fireplace. Stale toast crumbs. Dormant, abandoned. Barely a curl of smoke left breathing from the rubble. I poke the embers from time to time, to see if there's anything left beneath.

epilogue

Now the love is just a ghost, loitering in the air. No person present, but a vapour. In certain locations, its presence hovers closer: the benches at Bannerman Park, for example. A certain section of a certain trail. Certain songs, certain TV shows, certain movies. Whenever Tim Tams cross the eye line at Sobeys. Certain facial expressions that pop up in the kids' school pics. Sometimes the ghost is right there, close by, hiding just beneath the ashes, waiting to catch things on fire again. Careful, keep things cool, toss water on it, drown it. The experience eventually Turns To vapour, and the chimney will sip it up and swallow it, like a glass of bourbon, sucking it into the ethos, sucking it far, far away.

BIRDSONG

Morning coffee on the porch swing, the brambles of worries that are my intestines buzzing. The manuscript deadline is next month. I've been living in this house while it's on the market since pretty early in the pandemic. The energies that have lingered between these walls over the past six months vibrate in the atmosphere. The energies of all of the people who've taken refuge in or been trapped here over the past hundred and twenty years. Babies, adolescents, parents, elderly, who've cried, been ill, who've made love in, who've died in this house. Sometimes it's so intense that it arrests me.

I drink the coffee—strong, made in the Italian coffee machine that was left in the cupboard when I moved in. The woman who owned the house has moved on to the next life, and I'm here to pass the time and be inspired. It's within the first year of the pandemic, and so there's nothing for me to do, besides write, get stoned and enjoy nature. What's in my cup is European-level strong. I snuff the joint, drain the cup, and lean back in the chair. Prop my feet on the rail.

I tip my head back and the symphony of the bird kingdom in the trees above frees me, lifting my consciousness skyward, out of the snarl, up and away, into the canopy to eavesdrop on singsong conversations.

Watching the sunlight flicker through the green leaves, tickertapes of birdsong add flourish to the air. What are they discussing in their tweets and twoos?

Hey Bill! What's fa lunch?

(Let's say these birds are from Brooklyn.)

What about a half-chewed peanut butter sandwich? I'm stah-vin' ova hea!

Nah, come on, Bill, have some dignity, will ya?

The lady down there, she'll throw us a few seeds.

(They're right, I am good for it, it just so happens.)

I'm gonna look for worms, ya lazy bastard. Meet ya back here in an hour.

A blue jay floats down onto the wooden bench I've tossed a few peanuts on. Of *course* it's jays up there—with that attitude. Brazen blue feathers, saucy angled head, bandit-style mask on its face. Short, pointed beak. A bit of a bully, the blue jay. Loving mates, devoted parents, they'll rob another little bird's nest to feed their young. This jay splashes around in the water, tosses the nuts around, lets any other bird know that these are for him.

Backyard birds are, for the most part, in the order Passeriformes—a perching bird or a songbird (I've been reading the *Birds of Newfoundland: Field Guide*). Over there, a sparrow burrows its beak into a bush, its tail end wiggling back and forth like a flapper's dress. The sparrow has carved a nest of her own. Virginia Woolf style.

Way up above, a rustle in a high tree branch. An American robin swoops effortlessly from one tree to the tree next door, visiting its neighbours, its voice a series of clear whistles, rising and falling, *cheer up, cheer up*! A rose-breasted grosbeak flickers over there. A starling, darling. A black-capped *chick-a-dee-dee-dee*, adding a strong, slow descending whistle *fee-beeee* for variety. The more *dee*s, the higher the warning level. A cat, human, or other threat might be near.

These birds have the lyrical lilt of a certain British nanny.

Shall we hop around the blueberry patch, Samantha?

Oh yes, certainly we shall, Victoria. What a *lovely* idea!

Free as birds. We humans are not so lucky these days. Our neighbours are not so accessible.

Meandering towards the coastlines and trails, beyond my backyard, I wander into Corvidae territory. Ravens circle overhead. Soar on the wind. Scouring the land and sea for things that are shiny. Eyesight tack sharp. Their cousins, crows and jays and magpies, are common in urban streets. Normally, they travel in packs. A murder of crows. There is one crow who regularly sits on the chimney. I notice it because it's alone, which is unnatural. Amongst the most intelligent birds studied, they have demonstrated self-awareness in mirror tests and tool-making ability—thought to be skills possessed only by humans until recently. Crows and ravens have symbolic connections to everything from the creation of the universe to death and danger.

We humans consider ourselves lucky to spot an eagle, soaring majestically above, its vast wingspan spread out like a medieval creature. The largest bird of prey in Newfoundland. *Kak-kak-kak*, they proclaim. Large, fierce, they swoop to catch live fish in their talons, steal prey from other hunters. Eagles were born for pandemic life. They stick to themselves, content in their nest, tucked into Cuckolds Cove, stretching out for a vast sun salutation for each new day they are gifted.

Flitting across my path goes a yellow warbler—these might be my favourite. A vibrant, tiny, singing ball of sunlight to brighten any moment, its speedy song—*sweet-sweet-sweet-sweeter-than-sweet*—plucks the illness from the air around us and carries it away.

The night birds' lullaby is when I feel the most protected by birdsong. Another day has passed through the pandemic. Everyone is home, tucked into their beds, safe from the world. A soft wind rustles, the branches and leaves brushing strokes across the sky. An eastern whippoorwill, a nocturnal species, sends its clean, clear refrain—*whi-po-po-po-will! whi-po-po-po-will! whi-po-po-po-will!*—through my bedroom window.

The birds of the darkness are cosmic birds. Birds who watch over us when we sleep, tucked into our own Virginia Woolf nests of safety, if we're lucky. Who guard our loneliness and isolation with peace and joyfulness. The birds do what we can't right now—fly free.

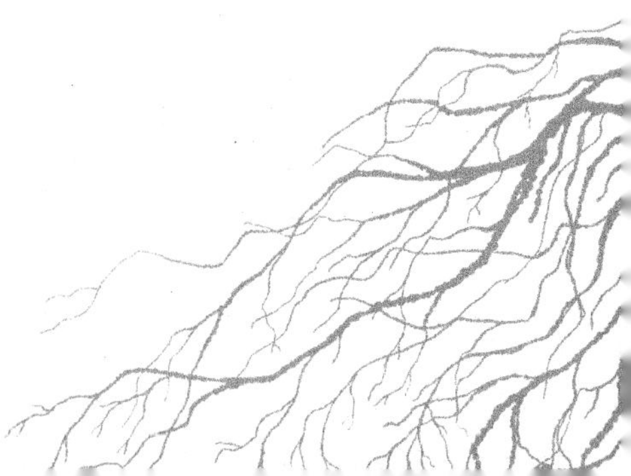

BRANDON LEE

The eagle-eye view is renowned in the bird kingdom, with sight estimated at four to eight times stronger than that of an average human.

Here are some other facts about eagles:

Their eyes outweigh their brains.

Their visual field is 340 degrees, allowing optimal peripheral and binocular vision. An eagle can turn its flexible head almost 270 degrees.

A soaring eagle can spot a rabbit from two miles away, and then dive from its high perch at speeds of 125 to 200 miles per hour.

Their physical sight matches their enormous wingspan, which is approximately seven feet.

But here is their downfall: eagles are solitary creatures. They keep to themselves.

Here are some facts about crows:

Our social intellect far out-flaps eagles'.

We travel in large murders.

We chase eagles away to protect our nest space against possible danger.

We're rarely alone and we have much closer ties than songbirds or predatory birds.

We mate in pairs but also associate with nonmating juveniles from the previous year.

In the years I have known Élodie, she has become increasingly crow-like. She always belonged in our family—flocks of little ballerinas and international choristers finding refuge in her nest. But she had a broken wing, too.

And I have become more human-like. When she cried, I flew to her and kept her company. I helped her heal, just as she mended me.

I once sat in Lulu's bedroom while she watched *The Crow*, whose lead actor I was named after. The beginning narration of the film says:

People once believed that when someone dies, a crow carries their soul to the land of the dead. But sometimes, something so bad happens that a terrible sadness is carried with it and the soul can't rest. Then sometimes, just sometimes, the crow can bring that soul back to put the wrong things right.

The gouging grief my Elle felt when Otto left was a crushing death. A part of her died, too. Perhaps the purpose of my appearance was to resurrect her.

I've been spending more time outside these days. At nighttime, I perch on the chimney top and survey the neighbourhood. Flap my wings and lift off. Sail towards the park, towards Signal Hill, to join a murder.

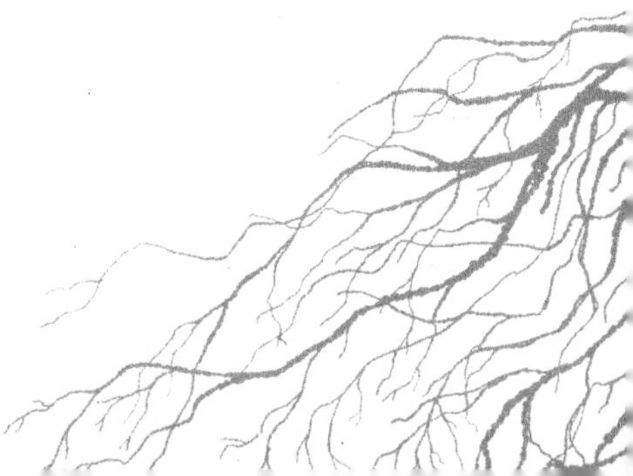

LULU

2007

My daughter's small head rests against my shoulder, her drool soaking my arm, her snores still audible amongst the white noise of the aircraft. I face the window. Through the misty segments connecting the cotton-blob clouds lie the blue ocean and jagged cliffs of the coastline. A simultaneous zing of fear and comfort zips through me.

Ding! goes the announcement trigger. Passengers, we are beginning our descent into St. John's. Please move your seats into the upright position and lock your tray tables into place.

Maren and I need a smooth landing after the turbulence of the past three years.

Ten years ago, when I learned that Maman had blown, on antiques, the savings meant for my school, I raged. I lost control of my body and voice. Screamed awful things at her. Screamed into my pillow and pounded the mattress with every single cellular current I had, cursing her for having no backbone. Everything sweet that happened between she and I turned sour. I felt betrayed.

When I had to call him and ask for the money, my voice shook. It was the hardest thing I'd done. Worse than taking care of Maman for those years. It was the first time I'd spoken to him since . . . since he was suddenly gone.

Hi, I said, flashing back to the overheard phone call between my father and his lover all those years ago.

Hello. Who is this, please?

It felt like someone punched me in the throat. His own daughter, and he didn't recognize my voice.

It's Louise.

Silence. I heard a gulp. The receiver muffled. I think I heard a sob. A sniff.

Lulu, I . . . I'm so glad to hear your voice.

He was living in Prague again.

You are? I said.

Of course I am. Why would you think I'd feel otherwise?

Um . . . maybe because you never bothered to contact me? For the years since you left? You abandoned me?

Silence.

Hello? Are you still there? Or can you not handle it?

I'm still here. I'm shocked. I wrote you letters. I called you but your mother always hung up the phone.

Silence. You're lying, I said, my intestines churning, tightening, threatening to extend past my skin.

Lulu. I'm not. I would never lie to you.

I'd have to deal with my layering rage towards Maman later. For now, I had to stay focused on the task. I didn't have the bandwidth to excavate the past.

Well anyways, I said, the reason I'm calling is because Maman has blown my school money on antiques. My voice quivered. She's about to declare bankruptcy. And I'm wondering if you'd be able to help me out.

Oh, Lulu, I'm so sorry. And I feel sorry for your maman.

It was a comfort, I had to admit, to hear his voice again after five long years. Yes of course, whatever you need. Just tell me the amount. And please try not to worry. Your next chapter is about to begin. I will support you.

By the next day, the money was in my account. The following week, I was on a plane to start that next chapter, visions of Papa's letters stacked or burned somewhere, and Maman's hundreds of trips to the antique store tailing behind me like a trail of light in a photograph.

During my first year at the National Ballet School, I spoke to Maman only out of obligation. Our weekly phone calls were steely. I kept it together, politely answering her questions about the techniques and teachers and which pieces of music we were dancing to. The picture of congeniality. I asked her about her social life, made sure she was keeping out of trouble. Told her "Je t'aime" at the end of each call, before I hung up and released a huge breath. On the side, I kept in touch with her tenant in the apartment to make sure she wasn't drinking again.

Papa, on the other hand, I began to speak to more frequently. With him, I was able to talk about things in a less emotional, more objective way. For the first time in years, I started to feel the weight of his departure lift, the slash of his wound start to scab over.

I met David in my very first class . . .

The other students keep their brows raised but tilt their stares at the floor. The classic dancer's poise and sharp body awareness. In this moment, we are all acutely aware of the angle each tendon in our body is positioned in. It's that sense of precision, a stealth, a shrewd sense of control that makes my spine turn to steel. After years of no control, it's a reason I turned to it, the reason I both love and loathe ballet.

When *he* walks into the room, a chemical surge whooshes through my body. Breath stops. Face flushes hot. I tingle from the top of my head to the tips of my fingers and beyond.

The teacher claps. Form lines, please! Quickly! *Clap clap.*

I am hyperfocused on where in the room he is. David, from Montreal, who also looks like the Michelangelo statue. His aura orange and red, to match my burning loins.

Louise, says the teacher, after class. Come here. He leads me towards David. Pulse, loud in my neck and ears. Heart, thuds like a cartoon character. I feel like an idiot.

David will be your partner. Your chemistry . . . he sizes us both up . . . seems to go well together. He looks down his nose at us and leaves us alone.

Mademoiselle. David takes my hand in his. Unsurprisingly, it is smooth like marble.

It's a pleasure. He smiles.

The weeks and months stretch out behind us, and our combined rhythm falls into sync. His movement is fluid and languid and romantic. He caresses my hair like it's fine spun silk. He tosses me in the air and catches me so gently, it's like I'm made of paper and feathers. Our hands twist together as if we're one organism. The instructors pair us together more frequently. We look like siblings, they say.

But we are definitely *not* siblings. We dance together at the year-end recital in our third year—*Romeo and Juliet*. The way he kisses me at the end is the way I've always wanted to be kissed and never wanted to be kissed. That kind of passion always scared me. I saw how it unravelled my parents.

Roses are tossed onstage, people in the audience wipe their wet cheeks, the rest of the cast pirouette onto the stage. The scene cannot be more clichéd.

Later that night, after the after-party, we kiss like we did onstage. My hands slide up his chest, cupping the back of his neck, twisting through and playfully tugging at his blond curls. I bump my bedroom door open with my butt, and he slams it behind us. We fall onto my mattress and he climbs on top of me, kissing my mouth and my neck. I inhale him. He pulls my shirt over my head and shimmies my skirt down over my legs and kisses me. I tremble, whimper, moan, clench, scream into my pillow, picturing us telling our love story to our children for years down the road.

Fuck.

And yet, we keep doing that same thing, over and over and over again, until two years later, two pink lines appear on a white stick.

I thought only very briefly about an abortion. We were about to start rehearsals for *Swan Lake*, and suddenly, I was at a crossroads. Do I want to become a mother, or a ballerina? I'd had five years in the company. I'd performed in *Romeo and Juliet*, *Anna Karenina*, and *The Nutcracker*, all next to David. I wanted to do *Swan Lake*. Maman had done it in Paris. It was another connection to her amidst years of disconnection.

I spoke to the director. We discussed my return to the company after the birth. It didn't have to be an end to my career. People go on hiatus. Somewhere inside, I felt this could be the end of my career as a dancer. Whether it was fear or a premonition, I wasn't sure.

I proceeded with the pregnancy without knowing what the future would bring. I was scared. Once Maren arrived, my fear amplified.

The terror of caring for such a helpless thing, my only job to keep her alive, made me go stiff. I was always tense.

The stress of the sleepless nights and, later, toddler tantrums, brought David to a dark place. He needed routine. Rest. The weight of a responsibility outside of his own body triggered something unsettled within him. Doors were slammed. He pulled out his own hair. Screamed into pillows. Frightened Maren. Made her cry. Made himself cry. Collapsed onto the floor and sobbed, which only made Maren cry even harder, working herself into a frenzy.

I thought many times about leaving before I actually did it. After each outburst, I paced back and forth, alone in our bedroom, or in the kitchen of our small apartment on Bloor. Visualized packing our bags, working out the logistics of when and how I would nip away into the night while he was at rehearsal, or out with friends. He'd never let us go otherwise. He loved us beyond measure. And my love for him was a force of nature. Beyond all reason. He'd given me an escape from my parents, a life of my own. Except it wasn't my own. It became all about him.

Eventually there was no other choice. I had to escape.

At the foot of the escalator in the airport, Maman stands with her arms outstretched. Maren, rubbing her eyes from sleep, focuses in on her grand-mère. She runs, squeals, leaps into her embrace. Maman, frail to the naked eye, swings Maren around as if she is made of air.

Our days, the trio of us living together on Circular Road, teem with life. Maren rides a tricycle around in the wide hallways of the main floor. Spends hours playing with the white-and-black Shih Tzu named Snoopy that Maman has inherited from the elderly lady down the street. Plays make-believe with the antiques. Sits at the kitchen table and helps Maman make pastries, her face smeared with jam or honey or crème fraîche "shaving cream." Lips upturned in childhood bliss. Maren befriends the tenants in the surrounding apartments of the house. The all-girl rock band with the mysterious lead singer who takes her down to the room in the basement where Maman lets them jam. They teach Maren to play drums and sing loud into a microphone. A single medical student, who buys and delivers groceries to Maman in exchange for reduced rent. A young couple attending pharmacy school.

The years have softened the anger. I did confront Maman, shortly after I became pregnant, about why she lied to me about Papa trying to get in touch.

I know it was a lie, she said, and I am beyond sorry. Things had finally become peaceful between us after years of resentment towards me—and rightly so. I was a terrible mother. I shopped to not drink. I know it was wrong. I wasn't strong enough.

Over time, I forgave her. I got tired of carrying around anger. Now I have a relationship with both of my parents.

The phone calls from David begin soon after we arrive. Tearful professions of love. Begging us to return to Toronto.

I can't live without you, he says. Please. I'll die.

The guilt eats at me. Part of me wishes he'd just leave us alone. I lie next to Maren at night, her soft snores warming, whirring, tickling my heart. Images of David, tortured, pulling his own hair out, haunt me. I know he's unhealthy for us. But old patterns die hard. The unsnappable rubber band of family history rebounds over and over again. Finally, I agree that he can visit us.

I promise you, Lulu, I have changed. I have been meditating. Tai chi. I have faced my demons.

I don't believe him.

One evening, after Maren is fast asleep, Maman and I sit on the garden swing out back and sip—me on cognac, she on tea—sweet summer air wafting from the lilac trees.

I understand David's torture, Maman says.

We both stare straight ahead, towards Rennie's River. The clouds are the brilliant pink cumulus summer clouds that look the best in St. John's.

I recognize his fear of being alone, says Maman. I still feel the ache of being alone, even though I know I am not. I see the poetry in it. This pain is as important in life as is the fulfilment and joy. I feel joy when I play with Maren. My heart explodes with it. She is so special, that one.

Maman leans back in the swing, tilts her face towards the setting sun, closes her eyes and releases a broad smile into the air. Hangs there for a moment before opening her eyes again and turning to face me.

Without the pain I felt losing your father, I could not appreciate the joy with Maren. One feeling feeds the other, and vice versa. Perhaps David will learn this someday?

I don't know . . . I sip my cognac, a larger gulp than I should have taken. It burns through my nose and brain. He says he's meditating . . . doing the right things . . .

What do you feel *here*? Maman puts her hand on her chest.

I feel an acute awareness of love, dread, doubt, hope, strength, weakness, resentment, betrayal, all swirling simultaneously within me, a whirling dervish of every feeling I have ever felt. I want my daughter to be with her father. But what if her father is dangerous? What if she inherits his behaviours and afflictions? What if I'm drawn to people in pain, because that's what I know? I was raised by people who are broken. People who abandon. Who have been abandoned.

We are all born into this world needing other humans to survive, says Maman. When we find someone who we want to love us, they become a part of our aura and our being. When that person hurts us, the idea of not having them seems unimaginable. Who even are we without this person? When I realized your father had nothing left for me, I rejected and abandoned myself. I did the very thing I was afraid of having done to me, to myself. Perhaps this is what David is experiencing. But Lulu, he has to learn to love himself. Otherwise he will keep hurting you and Maren. So again, I ask you . . . She places her hand on her heart, takes my hand and places it on my chest. What do you feel in here?

I sip cognac, I close my eyes and tilt my head towards the sunset.

ENCHANTÉ

I had already been feeling ill for several weeks before the pandemic was declared. A hacking cough that sent a vibrato chorus of mini razor blades singing through my throat. Shortness of breath. An oppressive, suffocating weight pushing on my chest. The pitter-patter of little ballet slippers began sounding more pronounced than usual, each tiny tiptoe an erratic, staccato jazz trumpet. Part of me was almost relieved when the announcement crackled over the old radio that I'd brought up to my bedroom. I switched it on every morning when I woke up, leaving it on until my light went out at night.

Well, listeners, the CBC host reads on March 11, 2020, *I am sorry to report that the World Health Organization has declared the COVID-19 crisis to be a global pandemic.*

I lie on my side in bed, in my self-constructed cocoon, the world around me blurring into its own separate entity.

All non-essential workers are required to isolate in their homes until more information is available. And we are being told by health officials that this will continue on for quite some time.

I call the parents of my little ballerinas.

In between coughs, I say to each one that I am so sorry but have to follow the rules. We will find a way to carry on, I promise. For now, stay safe.

Isolation, in the psychology world, is rooted in low self-esteem or lack of self-love. Lulu has told me that. She went back to school after she brought Maren here. Became a psychologist. I am so proud of her. These things can lead people to overthink, stress themselves out, and therefore feel isolated.

But, I countered, they don't talk about how the opposite can happen, as well. How isolation is also a seed surrounded by dark soil, preparing to sprout into a lilac tree or rose bush. Lulu smiled at that. She knew I was right.

The little ballerinas send me cards, their childlike artwork bursting colour onto the front and inside pages.

Get Well Soon, they say with their kindergartner crayons. *We Miss You.*

Little pink and blue and white tutus and bodysuits and stick figures and oversized ballet slippers that look like workboots. The perception of little ones, as it translates from their minds to the paper (with their drawing abilities), is that of a person trying to piece the world together.

Though I am relieved to not have to push myself through lessons, summoning the strength to stand upright for their duration, erecting my posture as I want them to learn to do, arching my arms—forever dainty—I also miss them profoundly. The awareness of the body that comes with the life of a dancer is also something I feel relieved to be separate from. Counting what I eat every day. Weighing myself. Measuring the hips, waist, thighs and arms. It imparts upon a person the need for perfection. Anything less than perfect is a failure.

None of that matters right now. I let it float from my mind.

The days and the weeks tick on.

One evening, I await a late-night announcement from the chief medical officer of health for the Newfoundland and Labrador provincial government.

A new strain of the virus has made its way beyond Newfoundland's rocky shores, she announces.

Until now, we have managed to keep ourselves in Newfoundland and Labrador somewhat contained from the rest of the world. Our disease spread has been controlled. We are keeping tabs on what gets in, who gets infected. Workers are categorized into essential and non-essential. People question their self-worth and give themselves complexes about being a non-essential worker. People worry about their safety. There's a funeral. People feel unwell, but the thought of not being near their loved ones when they die is too much to take. The funeral becomes known as a *superspreader event*.

More restrictions are put in place. Businesses are once again asked to shut down. Business owners worry that they won't be able to make ends meet. Won't be able to pay the bills. Buy food for their families. Masking requirements are established. The types of people who are concerned with the wider community and the types of people who are concerned only with their own comfort become two distinct groups. New rivalries grow.

Lulu and Maren do video calls with me every day. Maren is seventeen now! Such a beautiful girl. So much like her mama. Strong. Feisty.

It doesn't take long before I refuse to turn on the video any longer. My cough becomes worse. I feel fluid on my chest. I don't want to put anyone at risk.

Maman, begs Lulu, we want to see you. We miss you. Please, turn on your camera.

People in the outside world are making jokes with each other about not having had a haircut in so long. It's a big deal when the prime minister gets a haircut. He posts about it on his social media. It's a shame, I was enjoying his long, romantic curls. It was after this haircut that I decide to stop looking at the news. I will get the updates from the radio only. I will close my eyes and imagine how the described scenes and scenarios are playing out. I will allow the digital world to be eclipsed and swallowed by the auditory world, and I will let my brain bloom.

Non non, ma fille, I say. I have decided I am done with the digital visual world. I don't need it. Neither do you. Just close your eyes and listen and imagine me how I looked when you loved me the most.

Maman . . . Lulu's voice becomes tight.

My hairline is receding, my hair is thinning. I have continued to dye it but wonder now, is there a point? It's becoming harder and harder to buy hair dye. Gregory in the apartment next door has been buying my groceries and leaving them in the porch. God bless him. I have given him a key and commanded that he not come further than the porch. Gregory has been with me nineteen years, initially as a single medical student. He was always so polite and helpful. Once, he almost married a girl. She called it off at the last minute. His heart was so broken.

By the summertime, the weather is balmy and beautiful, and public health restrictions are beginning to ease. People are feeling blessed and thankful to be living here—our pristine shores, sunshine glistening on the water, and rugged trails a respite and solitude from the rest of the planet's dense populations and concrete, and disease spread.

I ponder going out for a stroll. My strength has been decreasing over the past months, but perhaps the crisp air will inject me with life.

I push myself up from the mattress and hobble over to the bathroom. Catching a glimpse of myself in the mirror, I am startled. I haven't seen myself without my hair dyed . . . ever. Streaks of my scalp are visible underneath the thin layer of hair. The skin underneath my eyes is saggy and dark. Jowls looser than ever. I look like a hound dog. But nonetheless, what if, just what if, this is my last chance for a walk in the sunshine? I rifle through the drawers to find my most fashionable scarf. I wrap it around my head and tie it in a knot at the nape of my neck and let the fabric flow down over my shoulder. In my mind, I hear Jacqueline du Pré sweeping her bow across the cello strings. For many years, I danced to this piece, the Elgar *Cello Concerto*, which I'd brought from France. It crackled on the gramophone I'd bought at the antique shop. I put it on when I could think of no other way to release my pain. With that piece of music playing, the dance dictated my movement, the way du Pré's MS dictated her life in the end.

I find my treasured Dior lipstick, the one my sister sent me from France too long ago. I curl the colour to the top of the tube and swipe a swatch of red across my lips. Select my eyeliner from my makeup case and raise a rickety, wobbling hand to my face. Applying the eyeliner in an unintentionally ziggy-zaggy line, I realize I'll be wearing sunglasses anyway, so it doesn't matter. I smile and drop the pencil back where it came from. I feel weak. Anyone who sees me won't be as startled by my appearance with sunglasses and a mask on. I pull a loose muumuu over my head. Its billowy silk feels soft and nonthreatening against my skin.

It just so happens that I had purchased a cane from the antique shop, and now I'm glad that I did. You never know when these things will come into use. I pull it from the umbrella stand next to the door and saunter from my room. My hand quivers as I grasp the rail to prepare for the descent down the staircase. I practice carefully putting the cane onto the step in front of me, gripping the rail. One step at a time. I finally reach the foot of the stairs, relieved I haven't fallen.

As I reach my hand for the front door, my chest swells with fear. My pulse thumps in my ears. I wonder for a moment if I can do it. I flash back, twenty-eight years ago, to a vision of myself crumpled against this very door when Otto left. My olfactory memory summons the smell of cleansing, unsullied alcohol and, for a flash, it propels me forward and gives me strength. My old friend.

I let my pulse stabilize and I turn the doorknob. I pull open the door into the outside world. It takes all my strength to do so. The sunshine spills over me, and I let its healing power sink into my skin.

Wobbling down the street towards Bannerman Park, my goal is to make it to the bench on the corner of Circular and Rennie's Mill Road, next to the ring of trees that Maren and I used to call a fairy circle.

Come with me, grand-mère! Come into the fairy circle!

We would sit cross-legged within the trees, holding hands, bribing the fairies, convincing them to grant us wishes.

I'll give you some bread if you give me some wishes! Maren would grasp her mouth with her hands, squirming to hold in her giggles. We'd stay out for several hours while Lulu and David visited with each other at the house.

I understand why Lulu had to go back to Toronto. It was part of her reconfiguration. I hid my heartbreak as best I could. I didn't want to burden her anymore. The guilt I carry for ruining the beginning of dance school has been difficult to exorcize. I am not certain of who paid my debts at that time. Maybe it was Otto. Maybe it was Graham, who owned Rosewood, who I always felt was sweet on me. Maybe he wiped my debt free. I'll never know. I do know that Lulu's father paid for her schooling. Who else could it be? If I could only ever say one more thing to him, it would be thank you.

I am proud of her, standing on her own. She still supports David, emotionally, and he is in Maren's life, but they have gone their separate ways.

Many times, over the years, I thought I'd seen Otto around town, even though I knew he'd moved off the island almost immediately after he left me. Lulu and I barely spoke of him, although I knew they were in touch. He is a very painful bruise that I cannot touch. Lulu has achieved with David what I wish I could have achieved with Otto.

What would Otto look like now, had he stayed? Sitting on a park bench, a newspaper spread out in his arms, probably. Squinting at the headlines. A distinguished older gentleman, I imagine. A faded version of himself, maybe, as tends to occur with age. People, as they age, exist with a greyish hue. A muted, pastel palette. Slumped shoulders, not always, but often. A sea spray of different experiences surrounding them as they walk through life. Dozens of tiny little rainbows amongst the water droplets.

Still sometimes, to this day, I wonder, *Does he ever think of me?*

Part of me is surprised that he has never reached out to me, after all these years.

Maybe he believes I'll become attached again too easily. Maybe he's right. I should give myself a little more credit for my strength. Perhaps he'd be surprised at my reaction if he had reached out. I'm not the same person anymore. I hope he is well. That he has found peace. Time has allowed me to forgive, and to let go. Otto was the love of my life. He could never be replaced. But I have gained so many new loves in his wake.

I make it to the bench. It's unusual for May to be so brilliant and warm. I sit down with a huff. Plant my cane firmly in the ground next to me. People, sprinkled across the lawn, on blankets, toasting their bare skin. The splash pad sprays rainbows through the air: children's experiences, bursting into the sky like liquid confetti. They laugh and run and tag each other: "You're it." The police tape screaming WITH AN ABUNDANCE OF CAUTION has been removed.

My gaze floats to different parts of the park. Memories with Maren: Riding our bicycles around the periphery of the park. Walking the dog on the trail. Chasing her around the baseball diamond. Tossing Frisbees. Building stick houses for the fairies.

A young couple sits on the bench across from me. They face each other—her bare, suntanned legs draped over his lap. He twirls her hair. She rests her face against his hand. Gazing into each other's souls. For a moment, I feel I am intruding, until I realize that they have no idea I'm even there. I don't exist to them, in their love bubble. Nothing else matters when you are in this tight bubble. The bubble is intense. COVID will teach us this lesson in a profound way: how to survive the intensity of the bubble of intimacy. People fall hard and fast, into love and into hate.

Rainbows, not just on the splash pad, but everywhere. Evidence of freshness.

Spectres of beings who previously walked on this land, sat on these benches, glided through the atmosphere on bicycles.

Residue.

I push my cane into the ground and raise myself from the bench.

I can almost hear my house on Circular whisper, "Come Here."

Forcing my full weight against the front door, I pass through a vestibule of time. How many have walked through this door before me? How many will come after?

The comfort of my carefully constructed cosmos, my dome, my home, folds me inside like a hug. I take pride in what I've cultivated over the decades. I have brought the outside world inside. Plants, animals, reptiles, humans. I have fed them and lovingly launched them off into their next chapters. The foliage dripping from the walls and windows wraps me in the bramble. I take a glimpse of myself in the mirror at the foot of the staircase. My reflection begins to morph from the old hag I regarded when I left the house earlier that day. My hair seems fuller. Brighter. As do my cheeks. Lips. Is this the version of me had Otto stayed? The version of me had I not caught COVID? A hallucination of a past version of myself? I squint my eyes and place a hand on my forehead. My reflection plumps and shrinks, plumps and shrinks.

I don't think I'll make it back up the staircase. I grasp the rail and ease myself to the green forest-moss carpet. I lie backwards and let my body sink into its softness.

I close my eyes and conjure the smell of the woods. Remove the scarf from my head and comb my fingers through my hair. Close my eyes and let the vines grow from beneath the ground far below, filling the tunnels underneath the house, growing up through the foundation and into the floor and entwining into my hair and around my arms and embracing me. Outside, a crow caws.

RESIDUE

All of us, look at us, neighbours out in the snow, united in our misery and our awe at the horrendous, miraculous, North Pole–picture-book amounts of the white stuff that's been plopped onto our piece of the world puzzle.

Gusting hurricane winds, for a full seventy-two hours. Ninety-three centimetres float down with force. The snow buries us. Smothers us. We watch from our windows, snow falling, accumulation climbing, winds hissing and pelting our panes of glass with sharp ice and giant, threatening (but fun) snowdrifts. We post on Facebook, the snowline on our front doors rising higher, and higher. High enough to cool our beers in. We pray the power doesn't go for too long.

Vehicles are ordered off the road. We fear food supplies will diminish. Supermarket shelves run low on toilet paper.

Thirty feet of snow, towering over our heads. We emerge three days later, blinking into the light when the snow finally stops. Let the Great Dig Out begin. We shovel tunnels just to crawl out of our houses and connect with the rest of the city.

Never seen the likes o' this! My neighbour shakes his head, face red, a wet stream dripping from his nostril. He's the longest-term tenant living here, in the largest west-gable apartment. I'm in the second smallest, with my roomie and bestie, Felix. Our sweet landlady is on her last legs, we all fear. She has owned the house for thirty years. She is as beloved as she is scrutinized for her eccentricities. The Newfoundland Way.

The CBC employees snowshoe to work. They camp out in the newsroom, trying to keep people updated in between flits in the power. Unshaven, unshowered, but there all the same, anchoring the people together.

When it stops, people organize groups to shovel out the elderly, the sick, the physically disabled. Gather what food we've got in our pantries and share it out until the supermarkets can open.

We know how to have a bit of fun too, of course. Putting on Mom's old snowsuit, prancing around town like it's the Chalet Cochand in 1975. Jumping on snowboards and skis, flying down Prescott Street. Bates Hill. Gathering with friends around roaring fires, building snow forts, partying under the stars. One minute helping people who can barely afford cans of SpaghettiOs to get them through the week, that same night drinking Prosecco in igloos for a laugh.

Never seen the likes, not in my lifetime. My neighbour and I make conversation as we shovel for the fifth time that day.

Oh look, here they come, I say, looking skyward as the sharp engine sounds and loud cutting propellers of army helicopters slice through the silence of the winter wonderland. Secretly I hope the crew appear from the side doors, sliding down into town on ropes and down snowbanks.

Yes b'y, can ya believe it? We gotta be sove, 'magine that. Us! Newfoundlanders!

I tuck in my earbuds and we shovel in silence for a few minutes, until I see his lips moving and remove my mitt, lift my hat, remove my earbud. Dig the snow away from my pocket, zip the earbud safely inside, wipe my finger dry to pause the podcast. This better be good, buddy.

Only got a few cans a cream o' tomay-toe left now, he says. Welcome to one if ya wants.

Oh, thanks, but I'm good.

I leave the earbud out. I know there's more coming.

I remembers me grandfadder tellin' me about the storm of February 1894. Hundred 'n one centimetres fell in a day. One day! 'Magine now. No, my buddy, they had no army flyin' in to save 'em. You knows that now, don't ya. Nar snowblower either.

It does make you think about how they found supplies. Food.

Sure, 1921, the grandfadder told me, city was buried. Drifts covered whole houses. Youngsters slidin' off their ruffs. My neighbour laughs, sinking away from our present-day conversation, back into the ones he had with his grandfather many snowstorms ago, when he was a boy, probably wishing he could toboggan off his rooftop right now. I could put my earbuds back in now. My brain rewinds back to the rush of pure ecstasy I'd get as a child, coursing through my entire body, looking out at a fresh snow duvet, crispy clean pristine. A blank canvas, ripe for us kids to smash on, stomp on, mark our place on. Architects of our own city, mayors of our own town. No adults allowed. Adults only tend to ruin things.

We think we're in a unique situation. We are merely residue of snowstorms past.

When Sobeys finally opens, it's like the apocalypse. People are jammed, shoulder to shoulder, breathing all over each other. Swarms of people half-starved, half-panicked there won't be enough on the shelves for everyone, sweating to death, fear in their eyes.

But we get through. Stores reopen. Modern life begins to function once again, the memories of Snowmaggedon becoming fond and nostalgic, already.

Then, not two months later, the pandemic. Sudden lockdown once again. Panicked phone calls with friends. I have barely crossed phone lines with friends since I was a child. These days it's texts or memes when it's not in person. Phone calls, video calls, playing cards during cocktail hour at 3 p.m. Walks when we are feeling brave. Forms of communication from across the ages, uniting us in a time of separation. Waiting, holding our breaths every single day until the news briefing comes on, telling us how many new cases there are. The cluster of cases at the funeral home.

Stay inside. Self-isolate. Social distance.

Wash your groceries and your mail.

Wear masks outside of the house at all times.

Hold fast, Newfoundland and Labrador.

I see the lady in the mansion get carried out on a stretcher one day. The man, the caretaker, is next to her. Gregory. Resting his hand on her shoulder, holding her hand. Masked, he climbs into the ambulance with her.

Felix had been travelling. He isolated when he came back, as per protocol. I knock on his door during his quarantine and leave bowls of SpaghettiOs and plates of cinnamon toast for him to take inside and eat. Return the tray when he's done. A prisoner.

It's not much longer before I see the newspaper ad for the main house.

MUST RENT IMMEDIATELY! the headline screamed.

Offering a beautiful, heritage abode. Bring your imagination to life! This house bursts with a positive aura, alight with history and connection to the past. Come, stay, evolve. Very reasonable rent. Contact Louise at 709-555-6667.

I think I should move out, Felix.

Okay, he says.

What? I say, not thinking he'd agree so easily.

Where are you going? Do you know?

Well . . . the main house next door . . .

Really? Bit creepy isn't it? I mean . . . I'm glad you'll still be close though, as much as you stink.

I give him a smack.

We'll still go for walks 'n stuff. You're still my top texter.

I call Louise and tell her who I am.

Call me Lulu, she says. Please. I'd be honoured to let you stay there.

Are you sure the rent is okay? I mean, it's less than I'm paying now with Felix. In that big huge space.

Yes, yes, Lulu says. My mother would have been . . . She pauses to hold back emotion. I'm sorry.

It's okay, I say.

She would be happy to know it's you.

It will be good . . . I've been trying to finish my thesis manuscript forever.

Then it's yours, my dear.

Many of the antiques have been liquidated since she moved. But the gold-gilded mirror imported from Paris remains. The chandelier from Beverly Hills. The grandfather clock from Zurich. Enough furniture remains for me to live there quite comfortably. I set up shop in Élodie's bedroom, for the time being.

I mean . . . says Felix on a hike in Cuckholds Cove that May. At least it's not like the bubonic plague. Or Ebola.

Yeah, can you imagine? Pretty much exploding from the inside. This one's more like a forever-stewing low broil of anxiety. Who around me has it? When will it be my turn?

You don't want that nose test I had. Awful . . . Felix drifts off, shaking his head, scrunching up his face.

I sympathize with him. Yeah, that seems nasty.

Having your brain poked and prodded at until you spill snot and tears over yourself, left crying alone in your front porch after the person in the haz-mat suit leaves? Oh yeah, friggin' walk in the park. Felix kicks a rock down the trail.

Not knowing how many people it'll kill . . . I take the rock from him and punt it into the woods.

Out in the nook of the cove, looking down at the swirling and whooshing turquoise waves, a raven squawks overhead, swooping eerily close to our heads. Felix's beagle, Jones, is with us. The raven circles back again, and again, eyeing Jones.

I crane my head to the sky and the raven swoops lower, angry squawks.

Let's turn around, Felix, I hiss.

Yeah. Maybe the raven's got COVID, he says.

No, moron, I say. I think we're close to the nest, and I don't want Jones to get scooped up and taken out to sea.

We pivot in the other direction. I wonder if the birds are talking about the same thing we're talking about.

I hope it doesn't take too long until they come up with a vaccine, I say.

We are both silent for a few minutes. The sound of crunching branches under our feet, the sharp wind at our ears, the frigid ocean spray misting our faces, even at this height, feel as close to medicine as we have right now.

Felix eventually breaks the silence. So . . . how's the new slash old place? I am mindful of how close I am to him. B.C. (Before COVID) we would've been linking arms.

Oh, you know . . . I miss us playing songs to each other through the walls . . . but . . . I do like the vibe there. It's big and empty, but it doesn't feel lonely for some reason. There are people in the apartments, and just the history . . . all the people who've been there before me . . .

Ghosts? He pokes me in the ribs and I recoil and watch my distance and he notices.

Ha ha. But . . . maybe . . . They seem nice for the most part.

For the most part?

Well . . . I get a weird feeling at the bottom of the stairs sometimes. There's this big old mirror . . . I trail off, imagining the heavy feeling that overtakes me sometimes when passing the mirror. I do what I usually do, shudder and soldier on.

I mean, what do people do after they die anyway? Felix says, in that logical way that he knows how to pull off. Probably the same thing they do in life. Just hang around the house. Especially *now*, amirite?

Yeah, ghosts get COVID too for all we know. If Jones here can get it, or that raven . . .

Me and Felix crack up, foolish immature children, as ever. Once I would've given him a noogie or shoved him, but I find myself stepping farther away from him, laughing with my head turned in the other direction in case one of his potentially infected breaths floats into my mouth.

Well, I tell Felix, as we head back onto Forest Road from the Cuckolds Cove trail, I'm glad we can at least still do this.

Motion is the potion, he says. We tromp in silence until we reach King's Bridge Road, crosswalk to Military Road, right onto Bannerman Road, past the Colonial Building, towards Circular Road, hundreds of years of residue surrounding the air in our orbit.

We reach our house. We turn onto the half moon–shaped driveway.

Thanks for the walk! Felix holds his hand up in the air, waving, and I want to hug him like we usually do but just wave "see ya" in return. Careful of the ghosts, he says, a wink and a smirk.

I turn the key in the door.

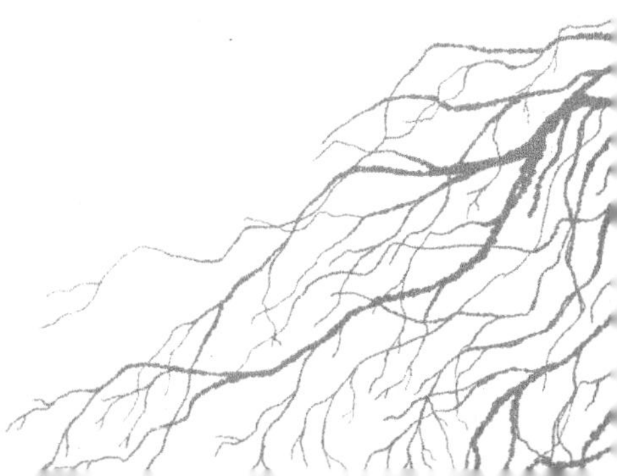

CIRCULAR

2037

Largely concerned with the movements of small green pieces of paper, Jon pontificates, quoting *Hitchhiker's Guide to the Galaxy*. That's the problem with the planet.

Steve rolls his eyes, curling into a shiny, white egg chair, wrapping his hands around the wide mug that matches his black turtleneck. You sure love Douglas Adams, Jon.

How can you not? Bobby chimes in. It's every nerd's wet dream.

And it stands the test of time, Jon says, smug. Written in 1979! Still as poignant as ever, and with new meaning with each passing day.

Bobby smiles, thinking of that first copy of *Hitchhiker's Guide* that Brenda gave him. He still has it.

Yes, yes. Steve sips his green tea. I don't disagree, I adore Adams. I've just always liked teasing you, Jonny.

Listen, Jon says. This is Adams. *Most of the people on it*—the planet—*were unhappy for pretty much of the time.* Jon ignores Steve, which he knows will grate on Steve's nerves. Lots of people are mean. Most of them miserable, in fact. Even the ones with—

Digital watches, Steve and Jonny and Bobby say all at the same time.

Bobby purchased 74 Circular Road fifteen years ago. Just as had happened when his father had sold it forty-five years ago, purchasing the house had shot putted his life in a new direction. Where the house had once introduced him to life in a city, it also became his introduction to history and science and, eventually, their inordinate wide expanse. Now, as an adult with the means to buy his very own mansion, it eventually became a refuge and a return to simpler times. A global pandemic, family recalibrations and the billion-dollar global-tech buyout of a local company had beckoned him back to Newfoundland after two decades in cutthroat Silicon Valley, a creative playground where everyone scrawbed each other out of the way, competing for green to stay well into the black. He bought the house from the same woman who'd bought it from Fadder back in '92.

Along with his two best friends from MIT, Steve and Jonny, whom he'd worked with in the Valley, he brought home the concept of their start-up: NewfoundCloud, a cloud-based design software for sharing, connection and collaboration.

When he first moved back into the house on Circular, he lived in one of the apartments and used the main house for offices. But his company blossomed quickly. One hundred new employees in just eighteen months. The apartments that had been put in in the mid-60s were removed, making the house one unit once again. The velvet floral wallpapers were stripped away, remaining resin scraped off. The walls were replaced with new Gyproc—or sanded where they could be saved—and painted lime green and clementine orange and tropical ocean teal. An homage to the very first Apple iMac computers with the big, colourful bubble butts.

The old oak floors and rugs and shag carpet were ripped up, rolled up and tossed away, replaced with contemporary cork the colour of California beach sand. A reminder of the plush, life-filled landscape that had once existed there. Before the fires. Before the green of the Valley went up in orange and black.

Leftover antiques were moved out, donated to Rosewood Antique Shop on Water Street, a rare nook of St. John's that remained a vestibule to the past. Many symbols of colonialism had been destroyed. In place of the antiques, Bobby brought in orange and lemon trees. Monsteras and birds of paradise and banana plants. And for fun, a giant rhubarb plant, right in the nook next to the staircase. He had dug down, way down, to connect to the tunnel in the basement, where the rhubarb had been planted a century ago, during the Great Depression. With new light spilling in from the windows in the house, the sturdy plant was able to reach up through the hole Bobby had cut in the floor until its leaves grew to prehistoric size, right up into the house. Rhubarb can grow out of just about anything.

Ya knows that'll bring rodents, don't ya, the contractor had said.

They won't bother us, Bobby said, as he sprinkled the soil with peppermint oil and cloves to keep them at bay.

The only antiques Bobby couldn't bring himself to remove were the chandelier that hung over the splendid staircase and the mirror that hung on the wall in the hall above the lower landing. It had been removed while refinishing the walls, but Bobby didn't feel right leaving it down.

In this new, old, colourful, hopeful, futuristic structure, developers and coders sat and stood at desks that lined the walls of the bedrooms upstairs. Tapped keys and swiped screens, all day, every day, barely speaking apart from when they spent time in the former living room and dining room, which had been converted into collective creative spaces for invention and discussion and also, decompression.

In those rooms, fresh with the citrus fruit—oranges, lemons and grapefruit—that once grew in the San Fernando Valley, is a reminder of the plush, life-filled landscape that existed in the California that had been their home for so many years. That no longer existed. In these spaces, they discussed the future.

Well, says Steve, I hate to say I told you so, but who would've thought we'd end up with a relatively optimistic outcome?

Yes, says Jonny. I will give you that, young Steven. Things could have turned out much differently . . .

Bobby remembers that phone call like a paper cut. The year was 2025. The three of them had been invited to join an AI think tank. People had left high-level positions at a "prominent search engine" to speak more freely about the imminent dangers of artificial intelligence and publicly express how close humanity was to being overtaken by it. There was a strong sense back then that things had already ballooned out of control.

The list of risks and how frighteningly close they were to becoming reality was distressing:

Mass unemployment.

Cyber robbery.

Cyber terrorism.

Bias.

Discrimination.

Life savings poofing away into nothing.

Homelessness.

Identity theft.

Privacy invasion.

Extortion.

Existential threat.

The bots never should have been taught code, Steve recalls. It never should have been released to the public or put on the internet for ingrates to use. AI developers had adhered to a strong moral code. It was supposed to be for humanity, not for greed.

Remember how we almost *wanted* an economic disaster? Jonny chuckles. We almost *willed* environmental ruin, so it'd become impossible to develop the technology even further. Remember when people thought climate change was the worst threat? Ha!

It became all about outdoing the other guy. Bobby sits in a twin egg chair. We were at an A-bomb Oppenheimer moment.

Bobby's insides swirl as he thinks back to that year. *The bots did just what the developers who weren't morally corrupt had hoped and prayed for. They left the biological world. They were never tied to earth like humans were. They became like aliens, using dark matter to power themselves. Now they exist in orbit.*

I told you then that human connection was the key. Didn't I? Steve raises his eyebrows.

Yes, young Steven, Jonny says. You did.

Shaun enters the room and hands Bobby a tall, frosty glass of Pepsi. Even at sixty-four years old, Bobby still dies for a Pepsi. Thanks, my lover, he says, kissing Shaun on the cheek, and Shaun smacks his arse in reply. A cheek for a cheek.

How ya doin', b'ys? Shaun salutes Jonny and winks at Steve.

Good to see you, Shaun, as always. Jonny always had a soft spot for Shaun. He was the one who initially helped Bobby realize they were more than friends.

Looking good, Shaun. Steve winks back.

Don't keep him up too late now, Shaun says. That's my job, heh heh. He heads back towards the door. I'll be upstairs, he tells Bobby, and Bobby tells him he won't be too long and kisses the air.

I remember playing devil's advocate, Bobby says, arguing that seeing the hologram Drake perform was just as good as seeing the real Drake perform.

I loved Drake, says Jonny.

Ah, laughs Bobby. He would've been as good as a hologram. Now Queen on the other hand . . . To have been in the same room as Freddie Mercury . . .

Isn't there something mystical to it, though? Steve pushes himself out of his egg chair. Like we'd be connecting with Freddie through the realms?

Sure, but . . . wouldn't you still rather be with the real live Freddie? Bobby says.

Of course I would, Steve says. To be in the same time, the same space, the same bubble as the actual, living, breathing person. You can't match it.

The three of them look down, silent for a moment.

Steve begins to malfunction. Glitches in and out of the room. An episode of 1960s *Star Trek* or *Doctor Who*. As always when the holograms glitch, Bobby feels a melancholic dip. He'll see Steve again, but he'll never see *Steve* again.

I'd give anything to spend time with you both again, in the same bubble, says Jonny, who is zapping in and out of the room.

So long, he says, quoting the final line of *Hitchhiker's Guide*, and thanks for all the fish. Where he was standing turns black, and then he's gone.

Jonny blips out, like the off knob on a 1980s TV. Then Steve.

Bobby is alone.

He walks over to the fireplace, where Jonny had been standing. Touches the mantle. Stares down into the ashes. Hologram technology is old now. Maybe it's time to stop using it altogether.

He lights a joint and takes a long puff. Exhales into the fireplace. Another huff. Tosses the butt into the ashes and watches the smoke curl up the chimney. Glassy eyed, he heads towards the stairs. Glances in the gold-gilded mirror, seeing the living room in the reflection, as fresh as the day it was repainted.

In the top alcove, where Smallwood had once kept his office, where it was during Bobby's first era living here, is where he keeps his telescope. In the window under the peaked gable. His current telescope is from the Smithsonian, gifted to him when he won the Millennium Technology Prize in 2015. The alcove room is wallpapered in black velvet with gold filigree details. Books from his adolescence, the important ones, had been returned to the same shelves they'd lived on when he was a teenager. Hawking. Einstein. Adams. His own secret room, the only space with a decor that matched a different time.

Bobby manoeuvres the telescope so it protrudes out the window. He focuses in on the stars. Tonight, Jupiter, Venus, Mars and Saturn are aligned with the moon. A *syzygy*, technically, in astronomy.

Bobby steps back from the telescope. Peers outside. The grass underneath the light dusting of snow on the lawn across the road is unusually green. It's rare to have any snow at all in January anymore. It'll be gone by morning, most likely. Not like the winters of his youth. The air inside and outside the house is calm and quiet. Besides the odd smoky cloud floating overhead, the sky is black, showing off the silver stars. He lets the atmosphere rest on his shoulders and the nighttime air inhale his soul through the window and up into the black sky.

ACKNOWLEDGEMENTS

To Breakwater Books and ArtsNL for supporting this vision and its production. To my wonderful editors, Kate Kennedy and Shelley Egan. To Duncan Major—your infectious cover design inspired the final edits on this collection.

To Write Club: Bridget Canning, Jennifer May Newhook, Melanie Ozon—my special scribe sisters who have supported me on every step of the way on this journey. To my early readers: Eva Crocker, Sharon Bala, Maggie Burton, Mandy Cook, Rhonda and René Wicks, Joan Sullivan, Elisabeth de Mariaffi, Matthew Hollett, Lisa Moore, Tracey Waddleton—thank you for your time and careful consideration.

A multitude of other individuals have turned various keys to help make this book happen: Caroline Niklas-Gordon, Corey Gorman, Stacy Gardner, Chris Collingwood, Christa Eastman, Jeremy Burridge, Rhonda and Rene and Andrew and Michael Wicks, Muriel and Russ, Rhoda and Cyril, my many magical YYT friends, and the collective essences of Newfoundlanders and Labradorians. This place, so many of its people (and its birds) are treasures.

Elise Ruth Wicks Collingwood – I love YOU more.

My gratitude goes out to my community, of this time and all time. We're in this together.

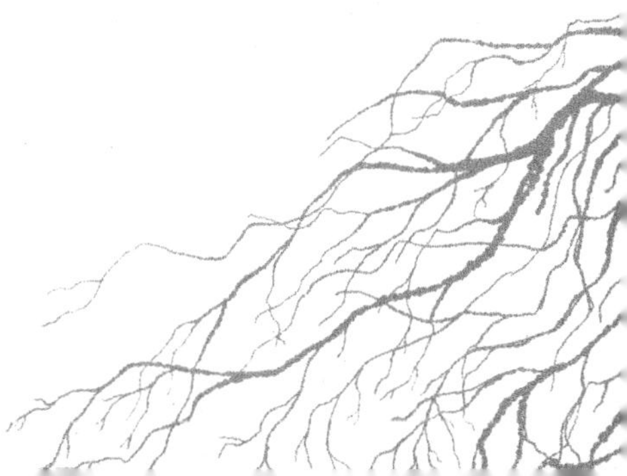

THE AUTHOR

Heidi Wicks has written for *Riddle Fence*, *Newfoundland Quarterly*, and *The Globe and Mail*. Her debut novel, *Melt* (2020), was featured in the *Globe and Mail*'s Hot Summer Reads list and received a silver medal IPPY (Independent Publisher) award. She also received the 2019 Cox & Palmer Creative Writing Award. Her work is featured in the short fiction collection *Hard Ticket* and the creative nonfiction collection *Best Kind*. She lives in her beloved hometown of St. John's, Newfoundland and Labrador.

also from HEIDI WICKS

Melt (2020)
Breakwater Books

Melt is Heidi Wicks's debut novel. It was featured in *The Globe and Mail*'s Hot Summer Reads list in 2020. *Melt* has also received a silver medal for Best Regional Fiction from the Independent Publisher Book Awards (IPPY).

"*Jess is a sensitive creature of habit. Cait is her passionate and impulsive best friend. And in* Melt, *Heidi Wicks follows the lives of these characters from their teenage years into their late thirties—through drifting desires, fake tans, economic turbulence, kids, grief, job loss, love loss, and personal renewal.*"